THE ENLIGHTENMENT OF ESTHER

JOSHUA BERKOV

Copyright © 2021 by Joshua Berkov

All rights reserved.

No part of this book may be reproduced in any form or by any electronic or mechanical means, including information storage and retrieval systems, without written permission from the author, except for the use of brief quotations in a book review.

❦ Created with Vellum

ACKNOWLEDGMENTS

I would like to thank my mother Francine Lamster, my stepfather Frederick Lamster, and my godmother Ellen Bradley for providing invaluable advice on the content of this book and on the cover design.

In addition, I would like to acknowledge the wonderful work that Chapel Hill Press did in conducting a thorough proofreading of my manuscript.

I would also like to thank Marlene Debo for conducting a final proofreading on the manuscript, checking for any errors that may have escaped the initial proofreaders, and I will forever be grateful for her continued encouragement of my burgeoning career as a published author.

CONTENTS

Chapter 1	1
Chapter 2	9
Chapter 3	20
Chapter 4	26
Chapter 5	34
Chapter 6	41
Chapter 7	48
Chapter 8	56
Chapter 9	64
Chapter 10	73
Chapter 11	82
Chapter 12	90
Chapter 13	99
Chapter 14	106
Chapter 15	114
Chapter 16	122
Chapter 17	130
Chapter 18	138
Chapter 19	146
Chapter 20	154
Chapter 21	162
Chapter 22	170
Chapter 23	179
Chapter 24	186
Chapter 25	194
Chapter 26	204
Chapter 27	212
Chapter 28	220
Chapter 29	228
Chapter 30	236

Also by Joshua Berkov 243
About the Author 247

1

Well, shit, I just hit another mailbox. This one's going to cost me big. It's the third one I've hit in the last month. My daughter's been trying to get me to give up my big, beautiful, beige Cadillac DeVille for something smaller and more manageable, ever since the right-hand mirror accidentally grazed a neighborhood boy on a bike. I told her it wasn't really my fault since the boy was riding his bicycle in the street where he shouldn't have been. And it's not like the boy was really even hurt. Just a little scratch! Though, you wouldn't know it by the way he was wailing and carrying on.

When his parents arrived at the scene, they threatened to call the police and press charges. Well, I wasn't about to let them call the police on me like I was some common criminal. So I offered to pay for the boy's college education, to which they kindly agreed and then admonished their boy for riding his bicycle where he shouldn't have been riding it. I could have saved a lot of money if his parents had actually done a better job of parenting him in the first place.

And ever since that minor little mishap, my daughter's been on my case about my need to adjust to my age. Well, her latest idea of helping me adjust to my age was to offer to buy me one of those new little Yugos that just hit the market a few years ago. She thought I needed a smaller car with better sight lines. Apparently, the new ones even have optional air conditioning! Of course, I wasn't about to drive up to my country club for my weekly bridge game in a tin can like that! No, I told my daughter that I thought she had been staring at those thousand points of light just a bit too long, and that I was about as adjusted to my age as I was going to get. She just threw up her arms in resignation.

But three mailboxes in one month, well, I was going to pay for this. I got out of my car and walked over to the mailbox to see just how much damage I had done. Yep, pretty bad. I thought about maybe running to the home improvement store to buy a new one and get it replaced before the owners found out, but I figured they'd probably realize that something had happened. They weren't likely to believe that the mailbox fairy just dropped a new mailbox on their property. And given that my car had already developed a reputation in this neighborhood for having an appetite for mailboxes, I figured I'd better own up to this one too. I suppose I could have fled the scene, but someone was bound to point their suspicion in my direction.

So up to the front door of the house with the recently damaged mailbox I went and rang the bell. The house was a well-kept brick ranch with a side-loading garage on the left side where the driveway was. I didn't really know these particular neighbors well, as they had just moved in last week, but I figured what better way to welcome them to the neighborhood than to offer to purchase a brand-new mailbox for their lovely used home.

A disheveled-looking older woman with gray hair sticking out in every direction and dressed in a tattered housecoat answered the door. Now when I say she was an older woman, I just mean that she looked like she was older than me. I'm pushing eighty myself, but I haven't let myself go like this woman seems to have done. I couldn't remember whether she was the mother of the husband or of the wife, but I knew she belonged to one of them. Not being sure whether she would remember me from the other day when I first introduced myself to all of them, I kindly did so again.

"Hello there," I started. "I'm Esther, Esther Kellerman, your new neighbor from just down the street."

"I'm, um, I'm," she started and then paused. "Sarah. I'm Sarah."

"Well, hello, Sarah. It's a pleasure to meet you, and I hope I will be seeing more of you. I tell you, the reason I rang the bell is because I had a little mishap with your mailbox," I continued.

Sarah looked around me to the mailbox, but with a slightly vacant expression on her face. She located the mailbox visually, and then slowly it began to dawn on her what I was trying to explain.

"Oh, I see," she said. "Come back later when my son is home."

But before I could respond, she shut the door in my face. Well, it looks like we have another nutter in the neighborhood. Just goes to show you! No good deed goes unpunished. Here I was, trying to do the neighborly thing and own up to my little run-in with her mailbox, and what does she do? She dismisses me!

I got back in my car, started it up, and headed towards

home. I was expecting company in about an hour for a monthly book club I belong to. It was my turn to host, and we were going to be discussing Margaret Atwood's *The Handmaid's Tale*. We had heard that some Hollywood studio was going to turn it into a movie, so we decided to reread the book, having read it once already when it was released a few years ago.

I pulled into the garage, got out of the car, and let myself into the house. I live in a Cape Cod–style home with a wooden exterior painted white, dormers for the two second-floor bedrooms, and a spacious master bedroom on the main level. The garage is in the back of the house, and the house sits on a corner lot.

Oh, and every wall in every room inside is painted in a bright, cheery peach color. My daughter tried to convince me that I might have taken my obsession with peach just a bit too far, but I wanted a fresh change after the drab colors I had always compromised on when my husband was still alive. After I made sure that he was securely six feet under the ground a few years back and wouldn't be around to protest, I redid the house to suit my own tastes.

Please don't get the wrong idea though. I loved my husband dearly, and I still miss him every single day. Joe was one of the kindest, gentlest men I ever knew. Always willing to help out a friend or family member in need. Never taking more than what he needed for himself. And he was funny, too, but sometimes you'd have to listen really closely because he was always so soft spoken.

Joe and I had just the one daughter, Phyllis. No sons to speak of. Phyllis and her husband, Bernie, have three daughters, but they're all now either in college or have started their own lives, so Phyllis and Bernie have been adjusting to having an empty house as of late. She offered to have me move in with them, rather than for me to continue rattling around this big twenty-five-hundred-square-foot house all by myself. But I told her I'd rather suffer the indignity of driving around town in that Yugo she offered to buy me than to move in with them. We all live in the same neighborhood in a suburb just outside Columbus, Ohio, and I thought that was close enough for all involved.

You're probably wondering how my beloved Joe died, though. Well, it was a freak accident. A few years ago, we had decided to celebrate our fiftieth anniversary with a trip to Italy, culminating in a three-day stop in Venice. That final day would have been our official anniversary, but sadly, we didn't quite make it. On the day before, we were enjoying a leisurely gondola ride down one of the canals when Joe decided to stand up to get a better angle for a photograph he was trying to take. At that very moment, a local resident threw a metal box out of her third-story window and hit Joe squarely on the head. He lost his balance and fell face first into the canal.

The operator of the gondola jumped in, fully clothed and paddle in hand, to try and rescue Joe, but he was too late. And since I was left in the gondola alone, with no paddle, I just floated away, calling out for help to anyone within earshot. I suppose I could have jumped out of the gondola myself, but well, I never learned to swim, so I figured I wouldn't be of much use. So, there I was, floating away from my poor drowning Joe, and there was nothing I could do to save him. And for all of this to happen one day shy of our official fiftieth anniversary! I didn't know which was worse. Losing Joe altogether, or forever having to tell people that we were married for 49 years and 364 days.

And it was quite an ordeal getting his body shipped back to the United States for a proper Jewish burial. We Jews are supposed to be buried as soon as possible after dying, so I was operating under a very strict timeline. I suppose I could have found a Jewish cemetery closer to where Joe died, but I really didn't want to have to make sure that I still had an unexpired passport every time I wanted to go visit his grave. Rather inconvenient, don't you think?

So, after expending a considerable amount of money and effort, I got Joe back to the States within twenty-four hours. I even had to resort to bribing some of the local officials, given that his death was officially a crime and under investigation. They didn't want to release Joe's body to me. But I don't think bribes are illegal over there like they are here.

Phyllis met me at the airport after I landed, and we both made the arrangements to have Joe's body delivered to the cemetery where we have our joint burial plot. She's a good daughter to me, and even though we may disagree from time to time about what's in my best interests, I know she loves me as a good daughter should.

I once remarked to her that the older she got, the more I could see myself in her. Well, she didn't like that so much. But just between you and me, it's the honest truth. It's the curse of getting older. We become more and more like our parents the older we get. We can try and fight it, but what's the point? It's going to happen.

Joe wanted nothing more than a graveside service, so that's what we did. The rabbi said a few prayers, and then the cemetery attendants started lowering Joe's coffin into the plot. This should have gone smoothly, but one of the gears on the lowering crank mechanism broke, and the coffin dropped the last three feet in one fell swoop. Well, Joe always talked about wanting to go out with a bang, so I didn't make a fuss. I could just picture Joe smiling down from heaven as his coffin hit rock bottom. The other attendees weren't as amused, though.

The Enlightenment of Esther

In the Jewish tradition, once the coffin is fully lowered, family members and close friends are supposed to take turns shoveling piles of dirt on top. I guess it's supposed to be part of the grieving process, the final acceptance of a death, but this too didn't go according to plan.

Phyllis and I got up to do our part, and then I gestured to Joe's older sister Rosalie to take the next shovel-load of dirt. She managed the shoveling part okay, but when it came time to throw the dirt onto the coffin, her hand slipped and the shovel dropped into the plot and landed on top of the coffin. Oh, she was mortified, of course, but I tell you it was all I could do to keep myself from bursting out laughing. You know, I think we all deal with grief in our own way, and for me at that moment, laughter was the best medicine.

Anyway, since there was no spare shovel to continue the ceremony with, I turned to the rest of the attendees and dismissed everyone back to my daughter's house for a memorial gathering, a Shiva in the Jewish tradition. Phyllis had ordered some platters to be delivered from Katzinger's Deli, and I had arranged for some desserts from a kosher bakery, also to be delivered. Phyllis had a friend of hers stay at the house while we were all at the cemetery to take care of the food when it all arrived.

Well, when we finally did arrive back at the house, there was no food. We later discovered that Phyllis had forgotten to pay the deli ahead of time, and I had apparently given the bakery the wrong date. Like mother, like daughter! So, Phyllis and I rummaged through her kitchen, cutting, slicing, and chopping anything we could find to feed the fifty or so people who were milling about, probably just as famished as we were. In the end, I think we did an acceptable job, given what we had to work with.

We did a small fruit platter, with grapes, cut-up apples, and strawberries. We managed a respectable cheese plate, with sticks of string cheese, arranged in a sunburst pattern around a center of crackers. We heated up some frozen mini pizza bagels, though we had to pick off the little bits of pepperoni, not wanting to offend our strict-kosher family members. Finally, we dumped a box of chocolate-chip cookies onto a platter and called it a day!

You know, it's hard to believe that Joe's been gone for five years. I still have nights in bed where I turn over, expecting to feel him sleeping right next to me. And then I wake up and realize he's still gone. It's at these times when I wonder whether I will ever see him again. I mean, I know I won't see him again on this earth, but spiritually speaking of course. Is there really a heaven? An afterlife? Or what if he was reincarnated? Or maybe his spirit is waiting for mine to join him, and then we both get reincarnated together. Like spiritual soul mates, jumping from one life to the next.

As I was ruminating on what's in store for me after I die, which hopefully won't happen for quite some time, the doorbell rang. It then occurred to me, after looking down at the grocery items still in their bags, that I had lost track of time and had failed to get everything ready for the book club. Fortunately, I knew which of my fellow book club members was at the door, as she was always the first to arrive: my aforementioned sister-in-law, Rosalie. I knew she'd help me get the refreshments ready, though to be honest, she's eighty-five years old now and not nearly as steady with a knife as she used to be. I'll just give her something, um, safer to work on. Like washing and arranging the grapes and berries that I had bought.

2

I opened the door to find Rosalie standing there as expected. Though age has dulled her beauty a bit, she's still a striking individual. She's about my height, five-foot three, with beautiful silver hair set in a permanent. I wish my natural hair color were as pretty as hers, but it isn't, so every four weeks I head to the beauty salon for an old-lady blond dye job. My hair almost matches the color of my prized Cadillac! Anyway, Rosalie was wearing a floral-pattern sweater, mauve-colored slacks, and sensible flats. I was in a royal blue pantsuit with patent-leather black pumps.

Rosalie followed me into the kitchen, where I showed her the predicament I was in regarding the refreshments, so she picked up a knife before I could stop her and started slicing up a block of cheese. That's Rosalie for you! She does whatever she sets her mind to do, regardless of whether she should be doing it or not. You know, Rosie the Riveter was originally Rosalie the Riveter.

Rosalie was married to one half of a pair of identical twins, and she had a one-night fling with the other half. I asked her if she knew which of the halves she was with during that, um, encounter, but she refused to answer my question. See, I was thinking that the other half could have fooled her into thinking he was her husband. Obviously, she knew who she had slept with after the fact, but I was never quite sure if she knew going into it which half she was with. I guess that's a secret Rosalie will take with her to the grave.

As we were preparing the refreshments, I told Rosalie about my encounter with that new neighbor Sarah. Now usually, when I have gossip to spill, Rosalie is right there lapping it up like it's mana from heaven, but she seemed uncharacteristically disinterested in this particular story.

I started to ask her if she was feeling all right, but then I thought better of it. That's a dangerous question to ask of anyone over the age of eighty. You never know whether you'll get a short response or a laundry list of all the ailments that person is currently suffering. Sometimes it's just best not to say anything and assume that the other person is doing well.

Rosalie finished slicing up the cheese, and I finished washing and setting out the grapes and berries. We used to enjoy having some wine with our refreshments during our book discussions, but one of our ladies had a little mishap a few years back involving a bottle of vodka and the bald head of her husband. She had to give up drinking after that to avoid being charged and tried for domestic abuse, so now we all have to suffer. It's not such a big deal when we're discussing a book we all really enjoyed. But when we end up with an absolute clunker of a story, the wine used to help keep the conversation going.

Anyway, just as we had finished laying everything out in the dining room, the rest of the ladies started to arrive. We all lived

The Enlightenment of Esther

within a few blocks of each other, so no one had far to travel, but that didn't stop any of them from driving their cars over here instead of walking. To be fair, though, we're all in our seventies and eighties now, and none of us is in perfect health. Muriel, the oldest of our group, can't read print anymore so she gets her books in audio from the Ohio Library for the Blind. How she manages to keep getting her driver's license renewed is beyond me!

Once we were all seated, we started talking about the book. Since we had all read *The Handmaid's Tale* once before, the conversation was really just a rehashing of our thoughts and feelings from the first go-round. Who was the most tragic character? Who was the most evil? How could such a society have really come about? Could this happen here in America? Oh, how I was missing my wine right now. Actually, a good stiff scotch would have been better.

As the discussion of the book was winding down, Muriel decided to drop a bombshell on the rest of us. She told us that her financial situation had become pretty precarious, on account of living much longer than she and her late husband had ever budgeted for. She said that she was going to start looking after a new neighbor a couple of hours a day while the neighbor's son and daughter-in-law were at work. Well, she was clearly talking about Sarah since there weren't any other new folks in the neighborhood that I knew of.

"Um, have you met Sarah yet?" I asked.

"Well, no, I haven't," Muriel replied. "But her son David and daughter-in-law Dianne seem like nice people who just want to make sure someone checks in on Sarah during the day."

Now between you and me, the idea of nearly ninety-year-old Muriel looking in on nearly certifiable Sarah didn't sound like a good idea. But I suppose it's none of my business. Maybe I just caught Sarah on a bad day today. I mean, we all have those. Maybe she was secretly entertaining a gentleman friend while her children were away, and perhaps I had interrupted them. That would certainly explain the disheveled hairstyle she was sporting when she opened the door.

"Well," I started, "I had a little vehicular altercation with their mailbox earlier today, so I went up to the door to offer to purchase them a new one."

"A vehicular altercation?" Rosalie asked, even though I had already told her about it. "I thought Phyllis told you to get a smaller car so you wouldn't have any more of these little altercations."

"Anyway," I interrupted, before Rosalie could continue. "Sarah answered the door, and I can tell you that she's clearly not a well woman."

"Oh?" Muriel asked.

"Her hair was sticking up every which way imaginable, and she seemed to be having trouble processing what I was telling her about their recently demolished mailbox," I replied.

"Well, David did say his mother was declining, but he didn't go into specifics," Muriel added.

I had a bad feeling about this. If David wasn't being clear with Muriel about Sarah's condition, Muriel was probably in for a shock.

"Did he at least go into specifics about what you would need to do for her?" I asked.

"Just to fix her lunch and keep her company for a while," Muriel responded.

"Dear, based on my limited interaction with Sarah, I think you're getting more than you bargained for," I said.

Here's what I want to know. Why didn't Muriel just come ask me for help if she was having money troubles? I would have been happy to pay her to fix my lunch every day, even though I was perfectly capable of doing it myself. My late husband, Joe, was a very savvy accountant and had invested wisely over the years, leaving me financially secure as long as I don't live past my 120th birthday. I think there's a lady in France who just passed 112 recently, but she's not looking so good these days. Doubt she'll make it to 120, so I probably won't either.

"Muriel," I continued. "Don't you think you should have actually met Sarah before you agreed to become her companion?"

"Hindsight is 20/20, Esther," Rosalie interjected before Muriel could reply. "For example, I'm sure if you had known you were going to hit that mailbox today, you wouldn't have been driving so close to the curb in the first place."

"At least no one has called my car the Carnivorous Caddy," Muriel added.

"You shouldn't be driving at all, Muriel," I responded.

"According to the State of Ohio, yes, I should," she replied.

"Well," I said, changing the subject, "perhaps Rosalie and I will come and help you out from time to time with this new career of yours. After all, you're a working girl now!"

Muriel tried to make a joke out of being a working girl by lifting up her bosoms, but with mixed success. They looked like they were melting in her hands.

"Esther," Rosalie began, "this really doesn't sound like something I want to do. Count me out."

"Fine," I said. "I'll help out poor nearly ninety-year-old Muriel by myself. Don't give it another thought, Rosalie. But I'm surprised at your attitude. Would you care to explain why you won't help Muriel?"

"I don't owe you any explanation, Esther," she replied. "And I don't owe one to Muriel either."

Rosalie can be a bit abrasive at times, even harsh, but this was extreme even for her. It seems to me that if I could overlook her dropping that shovel into Joe's grave five years ago, she could find it in her heart to help Muriel and me with Sarah.

"Fine," I said. "I won't mention it again."

As our discussion over the new neighbors wound down, most of the ladies made their way out of my house until only Rosalie, Muriel, and I were left. The three of us cleared the table of dishes and glasses, and I started washing everything while the other two waited to start drying. Yes, I do have a dishwasher, but I just don't trust that contraption with my better china. Would you?

"Esther," Muriel started, "thank you for offering to help with Sarah. I'm starting to wonder if I've gotten myself in over my head a bit."

"Oh, you're welcome, Muriel. It's no trouble, at least not for some of us," I said while shooting daggers at Rosalie with my eyes.

"Muriel," I continued, "what really happened? I mean, with your money. I don't for one second believe that you're just outliving your financial projections."

Muriel didn't reply immediately. She seemed to be gathering her wits about her before divulging whatever secrets she had been carrying inside of her. I felt badly for her, but there wasn't much I could do until she was ready for help. Whatever she needs, I'll help her with. Well, except for any vital organs. I'm not willing to part with any vital organs. We Jews are supposed to be buried fully intact.

"No, you're right, Esther. It's much more serious than that. Or at least more embarrassing," Muriel replied.

I suppose I should give you some background on Muriel's life. She and her husband had been married for sixty-five years when he passed away suddenly during a freak accident in their basement involving a frayed electrical cord and a puddle of water. This was just a few years ago during a torrential storm that caused water to seep into their basement. They were using one of those wet vacuum cleaners to try to get as much of the water up as they could, but they didn't realize that some sort of rodent had partially chewed through the cord. Muriel's husband was electrocuted and died instantly.

After the very unexpected death of her husband, Muriel had discovered that he had mortgaged their house and forged her signature on the paperwork. He apparently had used the equity in their house to cover up the numerous debts he had accrued over the years. Muriel had told me at the time that it wasn't really that serious and that she'd be able to survive on Social Security plus a modest stipend from their joint retirement investments. But it seems to me that whatever income she had was no longer enough to pay the mortgage and cover her living expenses. To be nearly ninety years old and not have enough money must be pretty scary for her.

But wait, what did she mean when she said it was more embarrassing?

"Muriel," I began, "tell me everything. How have you managed to find yourself in such a position?"

"Oh, it's all so horrible. My late husband had had an indiscretion years ago. I didn't know anything about it until he had passed away and the offspring of his indiscretion came knocking at my door, wondering why the checks had stopped coming."

"Oh my," Rosalie said.

"How old is this son?" I asked.

"Fifty," Muriel responded.

"So, let me get this straight," I began. "Your late husband's son is fifty years old and was still expecting to receive regular checks from him? Is there something wrong with the boy?"

"Not that I can tell," Muriel replied. "From what he told me, my late husband had agreed to continue writing checks indefinitely to keep me from finding out about the affair."

Sounded like extortion to me, but I wasn't sure Muriel thought of it in those terms. If it were me, I would have sought out a lawyer and put an end to it. Muriel is a different kind of bird, though, and would have been more likely to do what she could to keep everything hushed up. And true to form, that's exactly what she tried to do.

Muriel explained that she had continued writing checks to this son of her late husband's. She didn't want her late husband's memory tarnished by a scandal such as this. Personally, I've always thought that these scandals were very overrated. I mean, think about it. In a generation or two, no one still alive would even care that Muriel's late husband had had an affair. And it's not as if he had been a prominent political figure or a famous actor. He was a banker, for goodness sake.

"So how much do you have left, Muriel?" I asked.

"Not enough, I'm afraid. I still have his Social Security benefit coming in and his pension, of course. But it's not enough to pay the hundred-thousand-dollar mortgage on a house we bought for forty-two thousand dollars back in 1946, my living expenses, and the monthly checks to his son. Our individual stocks and bonds have now been completely liquidated, so there's nothing left to draw upon."

"I see," I said. "If you were to stop writing these checks, would that solve your financial dilemma? Or are you still going to come up short each month?"

"It's not enough, but not having to write those checks would help."

The Enlightenment of Esther

"Okay, then," I said. "One problem at a time. How about you and I ride over to your late husband's son's place tomorrow and explain to him that you can't afford to be writing these checks anymore?"

"Oh, um, well," Muriel responded.

"What?" I asked.

"There's something I didn't tell you. The son is biracial," Muriel confessed.

Rosalie rolled her eyes, and I just sat there, wondering what to say to this. So, Muriel's late husband had had an affair with a Black woman, and the two of them had had a son. And that son is fifty years old, meaning the affair would have had to have taken place in the late 1930s. Yes, such an affair would surely have been frowned upon back then. But times have changed. We're in the 1980s now, the late 1980s at that, and shouldn't we really be past having to talk about these issues in secret?

"Muriel," I began, "if Jesse Jackson could run for president and Bill Cosby can play a doctor on TV, then I think the world is ready to know that your late husband had an illegitimate biracial child."

"Well, I just didn't want it to be a surprise. That's all," Muriel said defensively.

"Good," I responded.

Why should I or anyone else care what this son looks like? The point is that he's extorting Muriel for money. There are extortionists of all colors and creeds. You know, I think I should reward myself for my worldly view about this with a big ice cream Sunday for dessert tonight.

"But," Muriel started in again, "we would have to go after I visit with Sarah, so maybe sometime in the late afternoon?"

"I have a better idea," I responded. "I'll come and sit with you and Sarah for a bit and then we'll go on to, um, what's-his-name's house."

"Peter. His name is Peter," Muriel added.

"Fine, I'll stop by Sarah's, say around 1 p.m., and then we'll go to Peter's from there.

Shaking her head, Rosalie said, "I think you're both nuts. And since I'm allergic to nuts, I'll be going back home now."

And just like that, Rosalie left. I don't understand how Rosalie can be so, oh, what's the word I'm looking for? Blasé. That's it. Blasé about all of this. I thought she'd want to help out a neighbor and friend in need. It's not like Rosalie has never been in dire straits herself. Maybe not financially, but her life hasn't exactly been a bed of roses.

Rosalie was the oldest of seven, six girls and one boy, my late husband. Their father had died suddenly in a car crash as their mother was giving birth to their youngest sister. He had lost control of his Model T and rammed it into a storefront window of a florist shop where he was probably headed to buy some flowers to celebrate the occasion. His death left their mother a young widow with no one to lean on for support. Rosalie dropped out of school and took a job as a seamstress in a well-intentioned but misguided attempt to help out financially.

Rosalie would help take care of her youngest siblings during the day, at least until they were old enough for school, and she'd do her seamstress work at night. She also helped with the cooking and cleaning. I believe this took a real toll on her development growing up. Can you imagine having to work that hard at such a young age? She was only thirteen, and I'm sure she would have appreciated any help she could have gotten then—which is why I'm so surprised at her attitude now. It just didn't make sense to me.

Rosalie then proceeded to marry the first man she could land who would agree to take some of her siblings in to lessen the burden on her mother. That's how Rosalie ended up raising the two youngest as if she were their mother. She never had children of her own as a result. Never wanted them. Well, it didn't help that her husband was sterile, but it seems to me that if she had wanted children badly enough, she could have found a way. Maybe a lover on the side who resembled her husband, and then she could claim to everyone else that a miracle had occurred! Oh, wait, she tried that. Never mind.

Muriel interrupted my little stroll down memory lane and announced that she was leaving, so I walked her to the door and told her I'd see her tomorrow.

3

I took my Cadillac to the dealership the next morning to get the right mirror replaced. The service department clerk informed me that they were having a three-for-one sale on mirrors, in case I wanted to stock up. I told him that while I was very appreciative of the offer, I didn't think I'd be needing more than one mirror anytime soon. He gave me a very quizzical look, which I chose to ignore.

While I was waiting for the mirror to be replaced, I went over to the pay phone to call Rosalie. I wanted to let her know I'd be over to Sarah's as soon as I was done at the dealership, in case she changed her mind and wanted to come over and help. She asked me if I thought it'd be a good idea for her to buy some stock in the company that makes car mirrors for Cadillac, seeing as how they were getting a lot of business from me. I told her she'd be better off buying stock in an adult diaper company. She hung up on me. You see, Rosalie has a slight incontinence issue that she doesn't want anyone to know about.

Anyway, once the mirror was fixed and paid for, I drove over to Sarah's, arriving just before noon, a whole hour earlier than I had planned. Muriel opened the door for me and then went back into the kitchen where she was fixing a turkey sandwich for Sarah's lunch. Damn, I thought, I should have eaten something before coming over. Who knows when I'll have the chance to eat today?

Sarah was seated in a recliner in the living room, staring at the TV. *The Price Is Right* was just about wrapping up. Apparently one of the contestants had just won both showcases by coming within one hundred dollars of the true price of his own. Well, good for him. Maybe I'll try to get on *The Price Is Right* someday and win a car that's smaller and more appropriate for my age, as my daughter would say.

"Hello, Sarah," I said.

She didn't respond, so I got in between her and TV and said hello again.

"Oh," she said.

"How are you doing today, Sarah?" I asked.

"Fine," she responded. "Who are you?"

"My name is Esther, dear. We met yesterday when I accidentally ran into your mailbox. I live just down the street. I'm a friend of Muriel's, and I thought I'd come visit with you for a while today. Maybe help keep you company."

"Oh, right, okay. Esther."

"Did you have a chance to tell your son about the mailbox? I do want to make things right. I feel terrible."

"Go to the doctor. That's where my son takes me when I feel terrible."

"No, dear," I responded. "I mean, I mean I am sorry that I ran into your mailbox, and I want to fix it."

"My husband will fix it. He just went to the store for some eggs. He'll be back."

Husband? Oh dear. I'm pretty sure her husband is no longer with us. I think I might just be a little out of my element here. I could tell yesterday that she has some problems, but if she thinks her husband is still alive, then she's in worse shape than I thought. I decided I'd just have to come back again later this evening when David and Dianne were home and speak to them about it.

"So, Sarah," I started, "tell me about yourself. Are you originally from this area?"

"No. My husband is."

Again with the husband. Well, she's clearly suffering from memory problems. I wonder if she's been diagnosed with a specific condition. But if she thinks her probably dead husband is not dead, then this is more than a "I forgot where I parked my car" situation. This is more of a "I don't know what these keys in my hands are for" situation.

Just then, Muriel walked into the living room with Sarah's lunch on a plate. I tried to communicate to her with my eyes that I don't think she's realized what she's gotten herself into here. But there's only so much you can say with a good, fixed stare. I'd have to speak with her about it later.

"Sarah," Muriel began. "I made a nice delicious turkey sandwich for you. I hope you enjoy it. If you would like something else, please let me know."

"Thank you," Sarah responded. "Um, what's your name again?"

"Muriel, dear."

"Oh, okay. That's right. Does my husband know you're here?" Sarah said.

"No, dear, but I'm sure he'll be back soon," Muriel responded.

As Sarah began to eat her sandwich, with some trouble I

might add, Muriel took me into the other room and explained. First of all, David was indeed home when I knocked on the door to offer to fix the mailbox, but he was upstairs doing some unpacking. Today is his first day back at work since the move, and the same for Dianne. They were in a real pinch trying to find someone to look after Sarah, and Muriel just happened to show up at the right time. She had come over to welcome them to the neighborhood, and they all got to talking. They shared their need for a caretaker. She shared her need for money. It was a match made in heaven, I suppose.

But they weren't completely honest with Muriel about Sarah's condition when she agreed to take the job. That much was clear. When she tried to correct Sarah on the alive-or-dead status of her husband the first time today, Sarah became inconsolable, so Muriel decided to just play along afterwards. She said there's no point in upsetting Sarah any further, and if it gives her some happiness or at least peace of mind to think that her husband is still alive, then that was okay with her.

"Muriel," I started. "Are you sure you're going to be able to handle this? If David and Dianne weren't honest with you about Sarah's condition, you should feel no obligation to continue on here. They have all but entrapped you."

"Now I think that's a bit harsh, Esther," she responded. "They were desperate."

"But something just isn't adding up here," I replied. "Why would they move here without a plan to take care of her if she's this badly off?"

"That I don't know, Esther."

"Well, I intend to find out when I come back over here this evening to discuss the mailbox incident with David and Dianne," I said.

"Let me know what you find out. I'm not sure we should even let her out of our sight this afternoon," Muriel added.

"What do you mean *we*?" I asked. "This is your doing, not mine. You leapt into this job, not me."

"Oh, Esther, I'm really going to need help with Sarah. I feel like I've been getting pretty frail lately, and this is just too much for me. She needs more care than I can give by myself."

"Well, I'm a frail old woman, too. Just slightly less frail and less old. No offense, dear."

"None taken, you mailbox assassin," Muriel joked.

"All right, Muriel, I'll help you out just until we have a chance to talk some sense into David and Dianne."

"Now, let's go back to the living room before Sarah wanders off again," Muriel directed.

"Again? Has she wandered off before? How long have you been here today?" I asked.

"Since eight in the morning. David called me late last night and asked if I could come for more than a few hours, meaning the whole day. I told him I had an errand to run later in the day, so he said Sarah would be okay for a few hours on her own. Well, that was a bunch of baloney if you ask me."

"Tell me about Sarah wandering off," I pressed.

"I had to use the powder room earlier, and when I got back to the living room, Sarah had wandered off into the backyard. Good thing it's fenced in and doesn't have a pool."

"Good thing indeed," I replied.

We made our way back into the living room and, thankfully, found Sarah just where we left her. She hadn't quite finished her sandwich yet, but she was working on it, slowly and methodically. I do think she would have had more success if she had tried to keep the sandwich in one piece, rather than taking out each component and eating it separately. But who am I to judge? I've been known to pick off the bread of a tuna fish sandwich just to get to the tuna. It's the best part, you know.

"Sarah," Muriel began, "is there anything in particular that you would like to do today? Would you like to go for a walk? Or maybe sit outside for a bit?"

"No, I'm tired. My husband should be home soon," Sarah responded.

"Dear, I think we have time for a little walk or at least some sunshine before he comes home," I offered.

"Who are you? I don't know you," Sarah said to me.

"I'm Esther, dear. Esther Kellerman. We've met before. Yesterday in fact," I assured her.

"Kellerman," she said. "That name. I know that name."

"Yes, Sarah," I responded. "I gave you my last name when we first met. But don't you worry. I'm not good with names either," I lied.

Sarah didn't respond. She started staring into space, lost in thought I suppose.

I decided that if I was going to have to stay longer than I had anticipated, I had better go home for a quick lunch first. I told Muriel that I'd be back in a half hour or so, but that she could call me at home if she needed me sooner or needed me to bring anything over for her. I just don't understand what David and Dianne were thinking, leaving physically frail Muriel to care for mentally frail Sarah. And not just for a few hours, but for the whole day!

4

I returned to Sarah's after eating a quick lunch at home and knocked on the door. Then I knocked again. And again. But there was no answer. I knew both Muriel and Sarah had to be there somewhere, but I couldn't figure out why neither one of them was answering the door. Muriel's eyes might be shot to hell, but her hearing certainly isn't. She should be able to hear me knocking.

After several repeated attempts, I decided I'd better walk around the side of the house to see if I could peer in a window to see what's going on. I was just hoping that the side window I remember seeing in the living room, on the right side of the house, wasn't included in the fenced-in backyard. There was no way I was going to be able to open the latch for the side gate.

Well, sometimes the best-laid plans go to hell in a handbasket. I managed to locate the side window, but one of my heels got caught in some mud along the way, and I nearly toppled to the ground. The only thing that saved me from a hard fall was the rod of a hanging planter rooted in the ground. I was just cursing Muriel under my breath for getting us both involved in this mess.

I managed to make it to the window, and you'll never guess what met my eyes when my gaze first fell upon the room. Muriel was fast asleep, sitting upright on the sofa, and Sarah was trying to do something to Muriel's hair. All I saw was a can of hairspray, a brush, and a hairdryer sitting on the end table, and then I saw what looked like a curling iron in Sarah's hands. Oh, dear. I had to think of something quick. I knew that Sarah could really hurt Muriel, especially in her current mental state.

So, I did what any self-respecting elderly woman would do in such circumstances. I screamed bloody murder. Well, that stopped Sarah dead in her tracks and probably woke up every corpse in a two-mile radius. Okay, so maybe I overdid it just a bit because the next thing I knew, neighbors from all over were coming out of their houses to see what was going on. I looked back into the window and saw that Muriel had thankfully woken up, so I shooed all of the neighbors away and signaled to her to come open up the front door.

When Muriel opened the door, I took a step inside, removed my muddy heels, and then walked with her back into the living room where Sarah was still standing with the curling iron in hand. It turned out Sarah had forgotten to plug it in, so I suppose Muriel wasn't in any real danger, unless you consider what would have undoubtedly been an awful styling job to be a real danger. Personally, I could see an argument for both sides on that.

"Muriel," I said once we reached Sarah and I took the curling iron out of her hand. "We need to have a talk."

"Oh, I'm so embarrassed. I can't believe I fell asleep," she replied.

"You're lucky I came by and that Sarah didn't have that curling iron plugged in," I responded.

Sarah fixed her gaze on me and then asked me if I had an appointment today. Apparently, she was all booked up and wasn't taking any walk-ins.

Muriel stared in disbelief, but I was starting to put the pieces of the puzzle here together. In Sarah's mind, Muriel was her client, and I was a potential client. She must have been a hairdresser when she was younger, or perhaps in a past life if you believe in reincarnation. I'd have to ask her son about this later. And I don't mind telling you I'd also like to give him a piece of my mind, a good laying into with some patented Esther Kellerman Jewish guilt. It works on gentiles too, just in case he isn't Jewish!

"Muriel," I continued, "did David and Dianne give you any tips on how to put Sarah to sleep for a nap? Is there any medicine you can give her? She's going to get wound up pretty quickly if we don't do something."

"Well, they suggested that I read to her. Her focus wanders and her mind drifts off to sleep," Muriel responded.

"Perfect, crack open a book and get started," I said, then remembering that she can no longer read regular print. And I'm sure she neglected to mention this little deficiency to David and Dianne before accepting the job.

So I told Muriel that I would do the reading. I then set out to find a book to read to Sarah, but my search didn't take long, as there was a book with a bookmark sitting on the breakfast table nearby. I brought the book over to the sofa, opened it up to the bookmarked page, and started reading aloud as Muriel got Sarah to sit back down.

My breasts were swollen with desire. I could barely wait to get him into my bedroom and rip that tight shirt off his muscular pecs and rock-hard abs. He followed me into the room and before I could turn around, he enveloped me with his bulging biceps, sending shivers of pleasure up my spine. I turned around and kissed him with all the force my quivering lips could muster, taking his tongue into my mouth as far as it would go.

A little voice inside my head was telling me that this book was not meant to be read aloud to Sarah. I guess Dianne likes reading trashy novels—the trashier the better, I bet. I was in such a rush to start reading that I didn't even bother looking at the cover. Understandably curious now, I closed the book and looked at the title, *Insatiable Izabella*.

"Esther," Muriel said, interrupting my train of thought, "don't stop reading. Sarah's not asleep yet."

"Muriel, she looks like she's well on her way to dozing off. But maybe I could go search for something more, um, appropriate."

"No!" Muriel nearly shouted. "Keep reading. Get to the good stuff!"

You know, when I woke up this morning and was thinking of all the possibilities of how this day was going to go, the idea of reading a smutty book aloud to Sarah and Muriel never ran through my mind. I mean, could anyone have possibly predicted that this is where I would end up this afternoon? I took a quick look around the room but didn't see anything else to read, so I reluctantly continued.

I ripped his shirt off with the hunger of a ravenous beast, exposing his beautiful, sculpted body. I wanted to hold on to his pecs like there was no tomorrow. But before I could, he pushed me onto the bed and began working to free me of the intolerable confines of my bra. Once my breasts were free, he cupped them, sending more quivers of pleasure through my whole body.

I reached up and started undoing his belt, desperate to get his pants off of him. I flung the belt to the floor and slipped his pants off of those sexy hips, revealing his bulging thighs and a burgeoning bulge in his central region. I . .

I stopped reading. I couldn't read any more and still maintain my composure. I looked up to find Sarah asleep and Muriel's eyes glazed over.

"Muriel," I whispered, "get a grip. Act your age."

"Oh, Esther," she responded. "Let me have my fantasy. Just because there's a little snow on the roof doesn't mean there isn't still a roaring fire beneath."

I was sure I had heard that saying somewhere before, but I nearly fell out of my chair hearing those words come out of Muriel's mouth. You know, growing old takes a lot of things away from you, whether it's the passing of loved ones or the inability to do certain tasks for yourself that once came with ease. But to grow old and still have dear friends you've known for decades is a true blessing—a blessing that I am grateful for every single day.

"Muriel," I said, "if you want to read more of this tawdry tale, perhaps you should call up your library and see if they've recorded it. Just let them know that Insatiable Muriel wants to read *Insatiable Izabella*. That's the title of the book."

"Oh, how clever of you, Esther," she responded sarcastically.

"Yes, I thought so," I said with a little smirk.

"Thank you for coming over today," Muriel added. "I don't know how I got myself into such a mess. How could David and Dianne think I could take care of Sarah? Do I look like a Mary Poppins for the elderly to you?"

"Well, no. But you do have that umbrella with a duck's head on it, and you've been known to just snap your fingers when you want something done," I teased.

"You're a regular Phyllis Diller," Muriel cracked.

"Look, I think we should postpone our visit to Peter's until tomorrow. It seems we have a more pressing problem to deal with—namely your incapacity to care for Sarah. I'll stay with you until either David or Dianne comes home. Then the two of us will calmly and rationally explain that you simply aren't up to the task. Did they say what time they'd be home?"

"David said he'd be home around five-thirty. Not sure about Dianne. I don't even know what they do for a living."

"Honey, I think they saw you coming from a mile away."

"What do you mean?"

"Well, obviously they were desperate to find someone to look after Sarah before they had to go back to work. Why they didn't already have someone lined up I don't know. But they didn't. And then you showed up on their doorstep welcoming them to the neighborhood."

"They asked me if I knew of anyone who could look in on Sarah during the weekdays, and silly me, I jumped at the opportunity."

"And you didn't think to ask to meet Sarah? I mean, did they even let you inside the house?"

"Well, no. They said they were so busy unpacking, so I didn't want to take up any of their time. I was just so grateful that a source of income had practically landed in my lap."

"Why, Muriel, didn't you come to me if you were having financial problems?"

"I'm a proud woman. I'm not in the habit of asking for charity. I was too ashamed, I suppose. I knew you'd want to know what happened to put me into such a situation."

"Well, yes, I probably would have asked," I admitted.

"So, there's your answer," Muriel replied.

"Well, we'll figure a way out of this mess together. Do your children know?"

"No, they don't," she replied. "How could I explain to them that not only did their father have an affair but that they also have a biracial half-brother as a result?"

"Dear," I began, "you and I are of a different generation. Our children don't have the same hang-ups over race, or affairs for that matter, that we do. Just look at Donald Trump and the affairs he's rumored to have had. Don't you ever pick up a tabloid? Or at least read *People* magazine?"

"But your daughter is younger than my children are. My youngest is nearly sixty. Phyllis is still in her forties."

Well, I couldn't argue with that. Even a ten-year difference might as well be a millennium as far as social mores are concerned. My daughter grew up with television. Muriel's children grew up with radio. My daughter was born during World War II. Muriel's children were born during the Depression. My daughter lived on her own before she married Bernie. Muriel's daughters both went from her home straight to their new husbands' homes.

"So, what shall we do with our time until David and Dianne arrive home?" I asked.

"Let's do a little snooping!" Muriel replied.

"Oh, let's not and say we did," I responded, not wanting to pry into their private lives. At least not yet.

It's not that I'm totally opposed to ruffling through someone else's belongings. I just want to have a little more motivation before doing so. A reason or a cause. For example, if I were to suspect that David was a serial killer who preys on old widows such as myself, then I'd probably be more willing to do a little detective work. But since there's no reason for me to think he's capable of murder—yet—I just wasn't interested.

"Oh, you're no fun. Live a little!" Muriel said.

"You're one to talk. You took a job without getting all the details. Look where that's landed you. And me for that matter," I replied.

"All right, let's turn the television back on. I think Oprah is coming on soon. I heard she's lost some weight!"

So that's what we did. We watched the television while Sarah continued to nap. She opened her eyes a few times, but was asleep again faster than you could blink an eye. Oprah did eventually come on, and she looked stunning, I have to say. I really should watch her show more often. Today, the topic was men, their secrets, and how they express themselves through their sexuality. I kept checking over to Muriel to make sure her eyes weren't glazing over again in a fit of fantasy.

After Oprah was over, we just sat and chatted for a while, waiting for David to return home. Sarah continued to go in and out of consciousness, which was probably a good thing, though I did wonder if we should have woken her up and tried to stimulate her mind a bit. We're all at that age where you either use it or lose it. And she didn't have that much left to lose, in my opinion.

5

I heard the garage door open and a car pull in at five-thirty on the dot. Well, at least I can say David is punctual, if nothing else. I had barely spoken to him when I had stopped by the day they moved in, hadn't even had the chance to introduce myself properly. Funny, though, I had gotten a distinct feeling that I had met David before, but I couldn't figure out where or when. Just old age catching up with me, I suppose. It might not be long before I end up like Sarah.

David walked into the kitchen from the garage and then into the living room where we were still sitting. He was tall, had a full head of black hair that was graying slightly at the temples, and looked like he was in very good physical shape. He was wearing a gray tweed blazer over a white dress shirt and black corduroy pants. I wasn't so sure that the tweed and corduroy went together, but since he didn't ask me for my opinion when he was dressing this morning, I didn't comment.

He was clearly surprised to see me sitting there, in addition to Muriel and sleeping Sarah. I suppose I'd be surprised too if I came home from a long day of work and found someone I wasn't expecting sitting in my living room. But I had a few things I wanted to say to him, and good decorum wasn't going to stop me.

But before I could, Muriel stood up to greet him, probably afraid of what was about to come out of my mouth. I was ready to lay into him, and she knew it.

"David," Muriel said, "I'd like you to meet a dear friend of mine, Esther Kellerman. She lives just down the street and offered to come help me out a bit."

David looked at me with a bit of shocked expression on his face. I didn't know what to make of this, so I just stood up to shake his hand. He looked into my eyes very intensely, almost as if he were trying to peer into my mind. This was a bit unnerving to me, I have to say. It's not every day I have this effect on a man. Well, at least not lately. When I was a young woman, I was known to have caused a few car accidents from men driving by to get a look and not paying attention to the other cars stopped in front of them.

"David Locker," he said, still a bit uneasy.

"Yes, we met the other day when you all were moving in. Look David, we need to have a chat," I began. "It's about your mother and the level of care that she clearly needs and that you have not provided."

Muriel tried to speak, but I held my hand up. Nothing was going to stop me from giving David a piece of my mind. But the more I looked at him, the more I couldn't get that eerie feeling out of my mind that I had met him somewhere before. Maybe he's got a twin running around somewhere. It just unnerved me. And let me tell you, Esther Kellerman doesn't get unnerved often.

I didn't really know where to start with regard to Sarah, but

I began telling him about the incident with the curling iron, and then I launched into Sarah's repeated mentioning of her husband, whom she thought was still alive. From there, I mentioned her little escape to the backyard and the peculiar way in which she ate her turkey sandwich for lunch. I had expected a look of surprise on David's face after hearing what I had to say, but I was disappointed to see that he was nodding, as if he was already aware of these issues.

"Mrs. Kellerman," David said.

"Esther, call me Esther," I replied. I had just given him a pretty intimate description of his mother's current mental state, so I figured we were past the formalities.

"Esther, then," David continued. "I'm sure by now it's obvious to you that my mother is suffering from dementia. Her doctor isn't sure whether it's Alzheimer's disease or some other form of dementia, but I'm not sure that it really matters."

"I see. And how long has she been suffering from dementia?"

"A year since we got the diagnosis, but probably longer than that. We didn't really notice it at first. We thought she was just becoming a bit forgetful. She'd forget to pay her electric bill, or she'd forget to take the trash out to the curb. Nothing major. We thought it was just old age."

"That could happen to anyone in our age bracket," I said sympathetically.

"But then we noticed that she was repeating questions within the course of the same conversation. We realized her short-term memory was faltering. She was still living alone at this point, and we started to get a little concerned."

Muriel nodded, agreeing that this was a sign that there were deeper issues developing in terms of Sarah's mental capacities.

"We started checking in on her more often," David continued. "She was living in a house in a town a bit west of Columbus, and we were living in Pickerington, southeast of Columbus. So I'm sure you can imagine it wasn't easy getting over there as often as we should have. We offered for her to move in with us, but she refused. We felt that the situation was manageable for the time being, so we didn't push the issue."

"So what changed?" I asked.

"My mother continued to deteriorate," he responded. "She kept burning her food in the oven because she forgot how to set the timer. I think she hid a lot of the burnt evidence from us. It was only last month that we even found out. Oh, and she also stopped fixing her hair. She was a hairdresser for many years and prided herself on the appearance of her hair. This was a big wake-up call for us. Funny thing, though, she won't let anyone else touch her hair."

"I see," I said.

"Don't get me wrong. My mother was still pretty lucid most of the time, but Dianne and I realized that it was becoming unsafe for her to live on her own."

"So your offer to have her move in with you became, well, less of an offer and more of a demand?"

"Precisely," David responded. "We would have moved her in with us where we were, but we had already bought this house and were just two weeks out from closing. So, we decided that the three of us would all move into this house together at the same time—she from her house on the west side of town and us from our house down in Pickerington."

"How did your mother react to this?" I asked, genuinely curious.

"Oh, she said it was up to us. She made excuses about not wanting to deal with the maintenance and upkeep of her home, but I think she was getting to the point where she was as afraid to live on her own as we were for her to continue living alone."

"Okay. Here's what I don't understand, David," I continued. "The woman you are describing is very different from the woman I had the pleasure of getting to know today. Seems like a lot of deterioration in such a short period of time."

"Yes, she seems to have taken a turn," David added. "We don't yet know whether this is a temporary phase yet or a permanent slide. We thought she was still in a mental place where she could adjust to her new surroundings, but so far, this hasn't been the case."

"Clearly," I said.

"We spoke to her doctor yesterday when we realized that she was getting worse and not better after being here a week. He said that this sometimes happens with dementia patients when they are placed in an unfamiliar environment. But he was surprised, given that my mother still seemed to be in an early stage of progression."

Muriel added that she was very sorry that Sarah had deteriorated so quickly and that she and I would help as much as we could. Don't you just love it when someone volunteers you for something you don't want to do?

"Perhaps if we had stayed in Pickerington and moved her in with us there, she would have adjusted better. She was already familiar with our house there," David continued.

"So you've been here a week, and Muriel was the best you could come up with?" I asked.

"Well, Esther," Muriel interjected. "They could have done a lot worse."

"I suppose a comatose person would have been worse, so yes, you are correct," I admitted with a smirk on my face. That little jab was for her volunteering me to continue helping without asking first.

David explained to us that it wasn't until yesterday that they really realized they had a problem with Sarah. She had had a pretty severe meltdown, saying she didn't know where she was or who he and Dianne were. I'm not exactly sure whether this was before or after I met her when I was trying to own up to demolishing their mailbox.

He continued to explain that the meltdown had occurred after they had hired Muriel to come over just for a few hours a day, which means it might have taken place after my little visit as well. But what I still didn't understand is why they waited a week to find someone at all, even if they just needed someone to check in on Sarah for an hour or two here and there.

Well, David must have been reading my thoughts because he then explained that the person they had found to just check in on Sarah from time to time during the weekdays had backed out two days ago. He didn't go into any further explanation, and even though I so desperately wanted to ask, I gave him the benefit of my doubt and kept my mouth shut.

Sarah woke up just then and stood up to join our conversation. I wasn't sure how this was going to go, and I could see by the looks on David's and Muriel's faces that they were feeling just as apprehensive as I was.

"Mom," David began, "how are you feeling?"

"Fine, dear," Sarah responded, seeming to know who he was at the moment. "But who are these old ladies with you? Go out and find yourself a nice girl your own age."

Well, at least she's still got a sense of humor.

"Mom, this is Muriel and Esther. They were visiting with you before you fell asleep, and they are going to come around every day to check on you while Dianne and I are at work."

"Who is Dianne?" Sarah asked.

"Dianne is a girl of my own age, Mom," he responded.

"Sarah," I said, "we'll come around to help you make your lunch and maybe watch some television with you. Would that be all right with you?"

Sarah didn't respond immediately, but I could see she was working through this in her mind.

"Okay," Sarah eventually responded.

"Oh, and maybe I'll try to get my sister-in-law Rosalie to come around too," I added.

"Rosalie?" Sarah asked. "I would love to see her. Haven't seen her in ages."

David looked at her sternly, but I didn't think much of this since I figured she had a friend or relative named Rosalie and was thinking of this other person by mistake.

"Now, David," I added, taking him aside. "We're going to help you out until you can find more suitable care for your mother. Neither one of us is really up to doing this on any sort of long-term basis. I hope you understand."

"Yes, I do, and I am very grateful to you both. Dianne will be too."

6

I left Sarah's that night, and when I got home, I called Phyllis and asked her to come over for a bit. She said she'd be over as soon as she and Bernie were finished with dinner. This day had taken its toll on me, and I wanted to, well, I really needed to vent. But more importantly, I felt that I needed a sounding board to figure out how best to proceed with my new career as a home health aide. Phyllis had been a registered nurse before she became a stay-at-home mother to their three daughters, and I figured she'd be able to give me some advice.

Frankly, this whole notion of Muriel and me taking care of Sarah, even if only for a short period of time, didn't seem like it would end well. I was hoping maybe Phyllis might be willing to help out a bit as well since their daughters are all out of the house now. But I probably should wait to see if she volunteers first before I ask her. And if she doesn't, maybe there's some way I can get her to think that it's really in her best interest to help. What if something were to happen to me from the exertion?

She'd end up having to take care of me, and I don't think she's ready for that phase of her life to begin just yet.

At about half past seven, I opened the door to find both Phyllis and Bernie standing there. Well, the more the merrier I suppose. I do like my son-in-law, and I think he's been a wonderful husband to my daughter and a fabulous father to their daughters. Plus, he has this unruly head of curly hair that just puts a smile on my face every time I see him.

You know, when they first got together, I kept buying him different combs, brushes, and products to try to tame that mane of his, but nothing seemed to work. Then, one evening when I was babysitting my granddaughters, I went rummaging through their drawers and found an entire drawer full of the very same combs, brushes, and products I had given him. All still in their wrappings. What was I looking for, you ask me? Hell, if I remember.

Anyway, I ushered Phyllis and Bernie into the living room and asked them if they wanted anything to drink. They declined, so I excused myself to the kitchen to fix a glass of scotch for myself. Joe and I used to have a glass of scotch every evening before dinner, but since he passed away, I rarely touch the stuff. Not because I don't like scotch, but because I don't want to become known as the crazy old neighborhood lady who drinks alone every night.

I returned to the living room, scotch in hand, and was about to fill them in on everything that had happened over the last day and a half. But before I could, Phyllis launched into me with another speech about my need to adjust to my age and get a smaller car. Admittedly, I was just going to tell them that I had dropped by Sarah's to welcome them to the neighborhood rather than admit to my third mailbox assassination in the last month. But apparently, news travels quickly

The Enlightenment of Esther

and Phyllis and Bernie were already aware of my latest murder.

"Mom," Phyllis started. "It's time."

"Time for what, dear?" I asked innocently.

"It's time to get a new, more manageable car with better sight lines. Three mailboxes in one month. How many total mailboxes over the course of the last few years? Are you going for some kind of record? Is it your new mission in life to replace every mailbox in the neighborhood before you die? Because this habit of yours is really eating into my inheritance."

I like how she threw a little humor in there, but she better be careful when playing with fire.

"Mom," she continued, "I'm worried about you. I'm worried about all of the children who ride their bikes on the neighborhood streets. I'm worried about the innocent mailboxes still left standing."

"Phyllis, dear," I started, "it's my newfound passion in life to beautify our neighborhood. Lady Bird Johnson planted flowers. I plant mailboxes. I would think you'd be happy that I've found a hobby I'm good at. Too many people my age are just wasting away in front of the television. Take our new neighbor Sarah, for example."

"Who?" Bernie asked.

"Sarah," I repeated. "She and her son and daughter-in-law just moved into the old Smith house down the street."

"Mom," Phyllis interjected, "let's stick to the issue at hand."

"Well, dear, Sarah is the issue at hand. She's the reason I asked you over tonight," I responded.

Trying to switch the subject back to my mode of transportation, Phyllis stated, "We're going car shopping this weekend, and I won't take no for an answer."

"Fine, but I'm making no commitment to you to actually

buy a new vehicle. Now, let me fill you both in on Sarah and the, um, situation I've found myself in."

"Situation?" Bernie asked. "This sounds ominous. But leave it to Esther Kellerman to get herself into a bind."

I didn't appreciate Bernie's insinuation that I have a penchant for finding myself in troubling situations but I decided to let it go for now. I launched into the whole ordeal, from my first impressions of Sarah yesterday to my expert opinions of her mental faculties today. And I made sure to include Muriel volunteering me to help just so that there was no confusion as to who is actually responsible for getting me into this fix.

"I don't know what to say," Bernie offered, unhelpfully.

"Well, I do," Phyllis said. "I'm concerned that you're putting yourself in harm's way. Your reflexes aren't what they once were. What if Sarah begins to fall? Will you be able to catch her?"

Bernie added that Muriel and I could be held legally responsible should something happen to Sarah while she was in our care. I told him that I didn't think David and Dianne were the litigious type, but to tell you the truth, he had a point. I hadn't considered the legal ramifications of my new career. Bernie is a lawyer, in case you haven't figured that out.

That said, since Muriel and I already agreed to help David out until he and Dianne could find a suitable replacement, I figured I was stuck for the time being. But maybe I could be a bit more proactive in bringing an end to this arrangement sooner rather than later.

"Phyllis, dear," I began. "Perhaps you know of someone who would be able and willing to care for Sarah. They wouldn't have to start right away, but maybe it would be better for all involved if someone younger and more able-bodied were to care for her."

"Sure, Mom," Phyllis replied. "I'll start making some calls tomorrow."

"In the meantime, you can come over and help us out."

"Wait, what?" Phyllis asked.

"Well, I know you two are very concerned about my abilities or lack thereof in caring for Sarah, so I would think you'd want to help out. You know, since my reflexes aren't what they used to be, as you so insightfully put it."

Bernie tried to suppress a smile, but he wasn't fooling anyone. Phyllis gave him a stern stare, and he busted out laughing at the new predicament she found herself in. She clearly didn't want to help me out, and Bernie knew it. But if she refused my request, then she'd look like her concern for my well-being wasn't completely genuine. Oh, what a tangled web we weave when we try to manipulate our elders.

"Mom, I'll see if I can rearrange some things over the next few days so that I can be on call in case of an emergency," Phyllis finally responded.

"What things? Your girls are all out of the house now."

"Just . . . things, Mom."

"Think of it this way, Phyllis. You help me and Muriel out now, and I'll help you out by being on my best behavior when we go car shopping this weekend."

"Can I get that in writing?" Bernie joked.

"Or better yet, in blood?" Phyllis added.

"Well, of all the nerve! You two think I'm that badly behaved in public?" I asked, genuinely insulted.

"Not on purpose, at least, I don't think," Phyllis responded. "But how could you forget that scene you caused last weekend we were out to dinner and the soup you ordered wasn't hot enough for you? You remember? You told the waiter you liked your soup hot like you like your men and that the soup you had been served was a little too flaccid for your tastes."

You know, it seemed like an accurate analogy to me, so why should anyone be offended? Some people are just too prudish for their own good. Then again, Muriel occupied the opposite end of that spectrum for sure. For me, I draw the line at overt references to sexual acts being performed, so my saying that the soup was a bit flaccid was still on the safe side of that line. Apparently, Phyllis and Bernie's line is not in the same location as mine, much to their detriment. It's not my fault that they were embarrassed by what I said.

"Well, be that as it may," I continued. "I assure you I will behave appropriately at the car dealership, unless they try to cheat me. Then all bets are off."

"All right, Mom," Phyllis said. "I will agree to be your backup. If something should happen, just give me a ring, and I'll be right over. But, Mom, please don't call unless you really need the help. That's all I'm willing to do for now."

"You won't come over just to visit with us? I'm sure Sarah would love to meet you," I lied.

"I have some errands to run tomorrow, so no. But you can call me on my car phone if you need me and I'll rush right over."

"Well, I guess I'll have to settle for that. Just don't stray too far away," I responded.

"I'll be around town, so not far at all," Phyllis assured me.

I know it isn't Phyllis's fault that I'm in such a bind, but I have to say I'm disappointed in her. I'm her mother, for goodness sake, and I've done my best to not be a burden to her in my old age. I don't ask much of her. Hell, I even refused to move in with her and Bernie so that I wouldn't become a burden. All I'm asking now is for a little help with an elderly neighbor, and yet Phyllis is being so uncooperative. This is really unlike her.

I looked at the clock and realized it was getting late. It's Wednesday night, and *Night Court* would be on soon. I never miss an episode of *Night Court* if I can help it. That judge is such a cutie. I asked Phyllis and Bernie if they wanted to stay and watch it with me, but they declined. Bernie had an early morning briefing, and Phyllis wasn't really interested in *Night Court*. She preferred watching *Doogie Howser*. Personally, I thought the whole premise of *Doogie Howser* was a bit far-fetched, and the lead actor was way too young for me to have any interest.

So, I saw Phyllis and Bernie to the door and then sat down in front of the television to wait for my cute judge to come on.

7

I spent the next couple of days helping Muriel out at Sarah's. And when I say I was helping, what I really mean is that I was doing most of the work myself. I love Muriel dearly, but she's far too old for this line of work. When you're younger, a ten-year difference in age isn't all that relevant in care giving. But when you're old enough to remember a time before sliced bread even existed, ten years in age makes a world of difference in your ability to just stay awake for eight hours at a stretch.

Muriel and I had worked out a schedule, since we had nearly ten hours of care to cover each day. Muriel is an early riser, so she would show up to Sarah's at 8 a.m. and leave at 4 p.m. I would show up at 10 a.m. and leave at 6 p.m. This allowed me the opportunity to speak with David and Dianne when they arrived home in the evenings, and it also allowed for Muriel to nap a bit during the early afternoons. I told her she might as well just go on home around lunchtime, but she insisted on putting in a full eight hours on-site since that's what she was being paid for, even if half of those hours were spent sleeping.

I, on the other hand, wasn't getting paid for any of this. Nope, I was doing this out of the goodness of my own heart. But I was also genuinely curious about Sarah's story. I wanted to know more about her life and about her late husband whom she thought was still alive. Unfortunately, every time I started to ask her about him, she just kept saying he'd gone to the store for eggs and would be back soon. I even asked her what his name was, but she couldn't remember. You know, I have many friends who would love to be able to forget their husbands, but I found Sarah's inability to even remember her husband's name to be quite sad.

At least she still seemed to recognize her son when he'd come home in the evenings. Dianne was another story, however. Yesterday, she thought Dianne was David's high-school girlfriend Suzanne. Today, she remembered Dianne's name but thought she was a nurse, rather than David's wife. Turns out she was partially right, though, since Dianne is indeed a nurse.

Dianne is really a beautiful woman, with shoulder-length brown hair, green eyes, and a warm and genuine smile. She arrived home before David today, so we had a chance to chat for a bit. I gave her a summary of Sarah's activities for the day, which consisted of eating, watching TV, napping, and a single lap around the backyard for exercise. I thought of asking Dianne about her reading habits and which authors and genres she enjoys most, but I thought better of it, not wanting to embarrass her.

I asked Dianne if she and David had any children, but she said they were childless, a conscious choice on their part. She said that, though they had discussed having children many times, neither one of them was willing to give up their careers to do so and they didn't want someone else basically raising their children. Seemed liked a sensible decision to me, though in my day, the wife was expected to give up any career for the sake of her family. That's what Phyllis did, and that's certainly how I was raised.

You got married, stayed home, and had children. I had always wanted to have more than one, but it just wasn't in the cards for us. We tried, and I did eventually get pregnant again, but I miscarried at five months.

Anyway, I started to ask Dianne about Sarah's late husband, but before I could get an answer, Sarah woke up in an agitated state. She had been fairly lucid most of the day, with the exception of thinking her husband was still alive, but now she was clearly having an episode of some sort. She didn't recognize either of us and started rummaging around the kitchen drawers, taking everything out.

Dianne had a look of resignation on her face, which I took to mean that this wasn't the first time Sarah had started deconstructing the kitchen. She stood up, walked over to Sarah, and asked her what she was looking for. Sarah responded by accusing Dianne of hiding her appointment book and started muttering about not knowing which clients were on her schedule for the day. With a bit of quick thinking on my part, I walked over and explained to Sarah that today was a holiday and that she didn't have anyone scheduled to come get their hair done. This seemed to calm her down.

I told Dianne to go ahead and put the kitchen back together while I continued to occupy Sarah's attention. I led her back into the living room and got her seated in the recliner. I thought about reading to her for a bit, but I just couldn't bring myself to pick up that smutty book again, and there were still no other books in sight. I know I could have asked Dianne for something else to read to Sarah, but I didn't want her to think I was being judgmental of her reading preferences.

So, I just turned the television back on and watched the evening news with Sarah. The news anchor was reporting on the recent conviction of Jim Bakker, that televangelist who had bilked his supporters out of a ton of money apparently. Thankfully, we don't have any such movement in Judaism. We don't have rabbis speaking on television, asking for large sums of money for amusement parks the way the gentiles do.

The anchor then did a piece on the death of Bette Davis, who had apparently died in a hospital in Paris today. I guess we now know the answer to whatever happened to baby Jane. I could see that Sarah was showing interest in this piece, so I quietly got up to speak with Dianne as she was finishing putting the kitchen back together.

"Dianne," I started. "We really do need to talk about Sarah's continued care. Muriel and I are not going to be able to keep this up for long. We're both well into our golden years, and Muriel spent the better part of the afternoon dozing on your couch. We both understand that Sarah has taken an unexpected turn for the worse and that this has put you and David in a bind. We want to help out, but frankly, I don't see how either one of us gets through a whole week of this without a break. I asked my daughter if she could make some calls to some of her friends still in the nursing profession, but so far, nothing has come of it."

"I know, I know," she responded. "And the two of you are so kind to help us out. I think I've lined someone up who can come on Mondays and Wednesdays. Nothing yet for the rest of the week though. Would you and Muriel be able to cover Tuesdays, Thursdays, and Fridays for now? Just until David and I can get someone else in?"

"Well, sure, of course," I reluctantly said.

I thought about how this would affect Muriel's income, but I realized that she'd probably still be making more than she would have if she were only coming in a few hours a day five days a week. And if Muriel puts up a fight, I'll just make up the difference myself. And if she won't take money from me, then I'll start paying for her lawn care myself. We both employ the same gardener, so it'll be easy to arrange.

"Dianne," I continued, "I do have a favor to ask you, though."

"Sure, anything," she responded.

"I would really appreciate it if you could provide some better reading materials in your home. I mean, for when I have to read aloud to Sarah to calm her down."

Well, so much for not embarrassing Dianne over her salacious reading habits.

"It's not that I didn't enjoy reading *Insatiable Izabella* to her, but Muriel's eyes were practically glazing over in a fit of fantasy."

Okay, so I just threw Muriel under the bus. Eh, she'll live. Dianne burst out laughing, and I had to admit, I had a little smile on my face.

"Sure, Esther," Dianne responded, still laughing. I'll run out to the bookstore this weekend and see what I can find. Any particular genre or subject matter?"

"Not really. Just keep the sex to a minimum. You know, for Muriel's sake. I'd hate to have to call the paramedics for her if her heart starts racing."

"Oh, does Muriel a heart condition?" Dianne asked. "She certainly didn't mention it when David and I first hired her. Seems like something she ought to have told us."

"No, dear, she doesn't have a heart condition. At least not that I know of. Her eyes are shot to hell, but not her heart."

Dianne shook her head, but I lied and reassured her that Muriel's eyes aren't really that bad. Fortunately, Sarah wasn't on any medications that had to be taken during the day, so there was no risk of mixing up medication timing or dosages due to Muriel's declining eyesight. Aside from her dementia, Sarah actually seemed like she was in pretty good physical shape for her age, whatever age that is. Whether she's closer to my age or to ancient Muriel's age, I really couldn't say, and I haven't bothered to ask. It doesn't really matter in the end.

I helped Dianne finish putting the kitchen back in order and then said my farewells for the evening. I was tired and wanted to get home to rest up for my big adventure car shopping tomorrow with Phyllis and Bernie.

Yup, tomorrow is Saturday, and I hadn't even had a chance to think about what I might be willing to purchase. I'd like another Cadillac, but I'd settle for a Buick or even an Oldsmobile. No Pontiacs or Chevys for me, though. I was long past the point of such mainstream transportation. A Chrysler or a Lincoln would work too, but Joe always preferred GM cars, so I never made a fuss.

I walked in the door to my house, and it suddenly occurred to me that this would be the first car I've purchased since Joe passed away. I knew I didn't really need Phyllis and Bernie to come along, but I still took comfort in knowing that they'd be there to help in case I get stuck with an absolute shark of a salesperson. You know, I can't believe I'm actually going to buy a new car. I've been putting it off for so long, but even I have to admit that taking out three mailboxes in one month was a clear sign that I needed a smaller set of wheels.

As I continued to ponder what kind of car to get, I started to think outside the box a bit. I've always driven American-made cars, and maybe it was time for a change. Phyllis drives a Volvo station wagon, and Bernie drives a Mercedes-Benz. I didn't think that a Volvo was quite right for me: too stodgy. And the Benz seems like such a pretentious car, which makes it all the more surprising that Bernie drives one. When I told him what I thought of his car, he said it was more of an investment than a showpiece. He informed me that Mercedes-Benz built its cars to last a good four hundred thousand miles, and this was why he bought it. Between you and me, I wasn't buying it.

I sat down to watch some television after I ate my dinner, and wouldn't you know it, a car commercial came on. The commercial was for Saab and featured a sporty-looking two-door in silver. The narrator asks, "What becomes of the brokenhearted?" He responds to his own question by saying that the smart ones buy a Saab. Well, I wasn't exactly brokenhearted anymore. After all, it's been five years since Joe passed. But I'd like to think that I'm one of the smart ones the narrator was referring to. I think we'll definitely be visiting the Saab dealership tomorrow, among others.

Before turning in for bed, I called Rosalie to see if she wanted to tag along with us tomorrow. Her car is getting on in years, and she could use a downsizing as well. Granted she hasn't hit as many mailboxes as I have, but her car sustained some damage last month when she backed it into a fire hydrant when pulling out of her driveway. She veered off the driveway and onto the grass just a bit too far. It's a modern-day miracle that she didn't burst the hydrant open.

Rosalie accepted my invitation, and I told her to be here at 10 a.m. sharp. Bernie and Phyllis were going to come by, and Bernie was going to drive us all to the various dealerships in my

Cadillac. I figured he'd want to drive his flashy Mercedes around, but he said we needed to take my car so that we'd have it to offer as a trade-in. I guess it's a good thing I got that mirror replaced after all. I'd hate for the dealerships to think the car had been in any accidents!

8

I woke up the next morning and started my morning routine. I put a pot of coffee on and put some bread in the toaster. Just as I was sitting down to eat, the phone rang. I wasn't expecting any calls this early, but I figured I might as well see who was calling. Oh, if only I had a phone that could show me who's calling before I pick up the receiver. I've read about this feature in the news recently, but it hasn't been made available here yet. Maybe someday before I die, I'll be able to screen my calls, but that day hasn't arrived yet.

So, I answered the phone to hear Muriel's voice on the other end.

"Esther, dear," she began. "I hope it's not too early to call, but I wanted to see if you were available today to go over to Peter's and get this check business straightened out."

"I'm sorry, Muriel, but I don't think I can. I know this'll come as a real shock to you, but I have decided to go car shopping today. Rosalie will be here at ten, and Bernie and Phyllis too. Bernie will drive us all in my car so I can trade it in if I find something I want to purchase."

"Wow, I never thought I'd live to see the day when Esther Kellerman would give up her prized 1982 Cadillac Deville."

"Well, I figured since I'm a working girl again, I might as well have a new set of wheels to match."

"Maybe I should think about getting a new car, too. We working girls could have matching new cars!"

"Dear, I hate to be the bearer of bad news, but I don't think it's wise for a woman of your advanced age to try to adjust to a new car. Before you know it, you'll be breaking my record for the number of decapitated mailboxes I've notched under my belt," I snickered.

"So, what are you going to get?" Muriel asked, ignoring my little jab at her.

"I'm not sure yet. We're going to drive down Morse Road and stop at several dealerships. All I know is that it needs to be smaller and more manageable for me."

"Get something sporty. Live a little."

"I just might do that. Oh, before I forget, I meant to call you last night to let you know that David and Dianne only need us Tuesdays, Thursdays, and Fridays. Dianne found someone to come in on Mondays and Wednesdays. I hope you won't be too disappointed."

"Well, I suppose it's for the best. I really do need the money, but I think I'm better suited to being a part-time working girl."

"Yes, I quite agree. So, since we're not going to be working on Monday, why don't you and I ride over to Peter's then?"

"Oh, that would be lovely. Thank you, Esther, for agreeing to help me with this. You're a godsend."

"It's no trouble at all," I said. "Anyway, I need to start getting ready for my car shopping adventure. Let's talk tomorrow and set a time for Monday. Okay?"

"Sounds good. Oh, let me know what kind of car you get."

I told her that I would. We said our good-byes, and I busied myself with getting ready for the day ahead. I took a shower, fixed my hair, and walked into my closet to figure out what to wear. Oh, if only I had a good power suit. It might ward off any salespeople who might try to take advantage of this poor old widow. Well, not so poor, I suppose. But still, I want to make sure I pay a fair price for whatever car I end up purchasing.

I settled on a red St. John knit suit that I've had for a few years. It's not exactly form fitting, but when you get to be my age, your form isn't quite where it used to be. The extra material does a fine job of leaving my true form to the imagination. It's got a white-and-red-trimmed collar, sleeves that hit just below the elbow, and the skirt hits just below the knees. Oh, and I've matching red and white heels. I've been told that red is the color of power, so I figured this suit was as close as I was going to get to an actual power suit.

All dressed, I walked back into the living room and was going to do a little bit of reading, but the doorbell rang. Of course, I knew who it was: Rosalie, early as usual. After all these years, I don't know why I haven't learned to tell her to come thirty minutes after when I really want her to show up. That way she'd be on time instead of thirty minutes early. I know she's got a Type A personality, and there have certainly been situations where I was glad for it, but sometimes she takes punctuality to an extreme.

I opened the door to find Rosalie standing there, dressed in a crisp royal-blue sweater, black slacks, and black flats. Sensible, if a bit predictable. I could tell by the look on her face that she was surprised I had gotten myself so gussied up just to go

The Enlightenment of Esther

car shopping. But she didn't say anything, didn't need to. Her eyes spoke volumes.

We made our way to the living room and sat down to chat while we waited for Bernie and Phyllis to show up. I started to fill Rosalie in on how the last couple of days had gone at Sarah's, but she seemed totally disinterested in what I was saying. I droned on for a while, and I could just see Rosalie getting more and more perturbed. But I couldn't figure out why, and I still had no idea why she wasn't willing to help us out with Sarah. It just made no sense to me. I was at a total loss.

"Rosalie," I finally said, "you look like you're about to spit nails at me, so come on, out with it."

"Esther," she began, "from what I gather, Sarah's got dementia. Am I right?"

I nodded and told her we could really use her help, and that I had hoped she would reconsider.

"Why would you think I'd put myself in the position of caretaker for someone with dementia again? My husband had it, and so did his brother."

"You mean your lover," I teased, perhaps inappropriately.

"Whether brother or lover, regardless, I took care of all of them. I have no desire to do it again, and I would have thought that you would understand that without me having to spell it out for you."

"Well," I replied, "no need to get testy with me, dear. I won't bring it up again. Hell, I won't even mention her name in your presence if that's how you want it."

"Thank you, dear," she said, regaining control of her emotions again. "Look, it's not that I don't feel for her, or for you and Muriel for getting mixed up in this. But I've done my duty to my husband and his brother—"

"Your lover," I corrected.

"Whatever! You know, Esther, I'm really starting to regret ever telling you about my little indiscretion. Point is, I've been the caretaker to more than my fair share of demented souls."

"Yes, dear, I know," I said.

You see, Rosalie's husband and his identical twin brother both came down with early-onset Alzheimer's disease. They didn't really call it 'early-onset' back then, but that's what they would call it today. It's such a devastating disease. Two otherwise healthy men in the prime of their careers very quickly became unable to care for themselves.

Now you'd think that, being identical, they would have been diagnosed at the same time, but things don't always work out the way we think they should. Her husband was diagnosed at age fifty, and her brother-in-law at age fifty-seven. The brother-in-law never married and had no one to take care of him, so since Rosalie's husband had already passed, she ended up taking care of the brother-in-law until he himself passed at age sixty-eight. Why her brother-in-law lived eleven years with the disease and her husband only six remains a mystery.

You know, I recently read a true story about a woman who took care of her elderly husband for many years, but within two weeks of his passing, she started showing signs of dementia. They say that if you are genetically predisposed to getting a disease, especially a neurological one, there's not much you can do to prevent it or delay it. But I'm not so sure I believe that. I think this woman held on to her marbles because she knew she had to care for her husband. But once that burden was lifted when he passed away, she let her mind go.

I think it's much the same with Rosalie's brother-in-law. He held on as long as he could, but he started slipping shortly after his brother died. He was a distinguished college professor, teaching physics at The Ohio State University, a brilliant mind. But he started having trouble preparing for his lectures and keeping his thoughts organized. Within two quarters, he took early retirement, as he struggled to keep up with the grading. He got his affairs in order, sold his house, and moved in with Rosalie.

He had enough money to go into a facility, but Rosalie wouldn't hear of it. You have to remember that, back in those days, nursing homes weren't as regulated as they are today. We've all heard the horror stories of inadequate care, but things were worse thirty years ago, and Rosalie wasn't about to let her brother-in-law suffer.

Because he lived much longer than her husband did, caring for her brother-in-law took a much bigger toll on Rosalie the second time around. She emerged after his death a much older, frailer woman. But who wouldn't after spending eighteen years taking care of two Alzheimer's patients? I suppose it really was insensitive of me to think of asking Rosalie to help out with Sarah. I really don't have any reference for taking care of such patients, other than my brief experience over these last few days.

Rosalie really hasn't had an easy life, though at least she's had some peace these last years. You remember how I was telling you earlier that when she sets her mind to something, she just does it? Well, after her brother-in-law died, she decided that she wanted to learn French, so she enrolled herself at the local community college and did just that. She even took a trip over to Paris all by herself about ten years ago, never having been out of the continental United States. Joe and I invited her to join us on our trip to Italy five years ago, but she said she didn't have enough time to learn Italian. She said she'd be damned if she was going to go to another country and be one of those entitled American tourists who doesn't take the time to learn the language.

It does my heart good to see that, even at eighty-five years of age, Rosalie hasn't lost her spunk. She can still tell someone off with eloquence and fortitude. You know, I probably don't even need Phyllis and Bernie to come along today. I mean, Rosalie can certainly stare down any unsuspecting salesperson who tries to take advantage of me. Just as I was about to pick up the phone to act on this idea, the doorbell rang.

"Well, hello, dears," I said as I opened the door for Phyllis and Bernie. "Come on in."

Phyllis went into the living room to say hello to her aunt, while Bernie took me aside to go over our game plan for how to attack the dealerships. He suggested that we start with the dealerships on one side of Morse Road and then cross over to the other side at the end. This way we wouldn't have to keep waiting to make U-turns. Seemed sensible to me. He asked me which dealerships I wanted to go to, but I said I wasn't sure, which was the truth.

"Okay, Mom," Bernie said. "Let's join the others and figure out which dealers to go to. I assume we'll be stopping at the Cadillac dealer, but perhaps there are other others you might want to visit. Maybe the Mercedes-Benz dealer?"

"No, thank you. No three-pointed stars for me. I prefer my stars to have six points in total."

"Umm, well, I don't think there are any carmakers using the Star of David as their emblem, but I'm sure you could have one custom made if you wanted. Just imagine, a Benz with a Star of David on its hood." Bernie laughed.

"That'll show the Germans!" I responded.

"Oh, you are definitely your daughter's mother. She gave me hell when I bought my Benz," Bernie teased.

"It'll be a cold day in hell when I buy anything German made."

"Suit yourself. I think the Germans have atoned."

"Do you, now? Well, my mother's oldest brother stayed behind in Romania. He and his family were wiped out by the Nazis. I don't forgive easily."

"Or ever," Bernie added.

I decided that I was done talking about the past, so I just walked into the living room, with Bernie in pursuit. We sat down, and the four of us started talking about the various makes and models on sale now.

Rosalie thought I should take a look at the new Lincoln Continental. Phyllis said I should consider looking at an Acura Legend. I agreed with both suggestions and added that I wanted to stop by the Cadillac and Buick dealerships as well just to see what they might have for me. Bernie threw in his Mercedes-Benz suggestion, which earned him an icy stare from me.

After finalizing our list, we all got up and headed to the garage to get into my soon-to-be former Cadillac, and off we went on our adventure!

9

When we got to Morse Road, we realized that none of us could remember which dealerships were on which side of the road, so we resigned ourselves to a day of crisscrossing sides as necessary. I thought about maybe adding a few more car dealerships to the list, but I thought better of it. Everyone was taking time out of their day to help me buy a new car, so I suppose I should try not to drag the process out too long.

But now that we were approaching the dealerships, I was starting to have second thoughts about purchasing anything at all. My Caddy and I have been through seven years of memories. Good times and bum times. We've seen them all, and my dear, we're still here. But I'm about to say good-bye to the last car I bought with Joe. It's times like this that I find myself grieving all over again. Every time something changes for the first time since his passing, I feel a little deflated. It's like, with every change, I move further and further away from him and from my life with him.

When Joe passed away so unexpectedly, I was so consumed

with getting his body back from Italy and planning the funeral that I didn't have time to process my loss. It wasn't until the last guest left Phyllis's house when the shiva was over that I finally broke down and sobbed like I had never sobbed before.

Phyllis, Bernie, and their daughters were all there to comfort me, but they too were grieving. Joe was the quiet but sturdy rock of our family, and none of us seemed to know exactly what to do next. Phyllis had lost her father. Bernie had never had a great relationship with his own parents, so Joe was really a father to him too. And their daughters lost a grandfather who had spoiled them with love and presents their whole lives.

I had woken up the next day after a horrible night's sleep, and I couldn't figure out what to do with myself. I put on a pot of coffee and went to the front porch to get the newspaper. When I got back to the kitchen, I absent-mindedly started separating the sections out for Joe and me. He always started with the front-page news, and I started with the local section. We would then switch sections until we each had finished what we had wanted to read. So, when I caught myself doing this, separating out the sections, I just fell into a chair, weeping.

The phone rang while I was still in tears but I managed to pull myself together enough to answer it. It was Rosalie just calling to check in on me. I told her about the newspaper and that I felt like the rug had been ripped out from under my feet, sending me crashing to the floor. I didn't know how to get back up. Well, she got in her car and came right over. I just hoped she didn't think that I had actually fallen.

When Rosalie got there, I poured us both a cup of coffee, and we had a real heart-to-heart. I asked her how she dealt with the loss of her husband, her brother-in-law, and others through her life. She and Joe had had five other sisters, but one had passed away early in her adulthood. No one would ever talk about her. Whatever happened to her was a closely guarded secret that even I was not privy to.

Well, Rosalie answered my question by telling me that you just have to think about these things philosophically. She mentioned the circle of life and that everyone has his or her time to move on. I told her that some crazy lady from a third-story window in Venice had decided it was time for Joe to move on, not God nor any other supreme being with a master plan. It just didn't seem fair. How Joe's life could come to such an unceremonious end I couldn't accept.

Those first days and weeks were some of the hardest of my life, but slowly I came to realize the wisdom in Rosalie's words. If Joe had lived, perhaps his fate could have been much worse. He could have developed Parkinson's disease, or he could have ended up like Sarah, or like Rosalie's husband and brother-in-law. Part of me still felt like I had been robbed of the elderly years I had dreamed of, but I slowly began to accept my new life as a widow.

I rejoined my bridge club after several months of not attending, and I began to read again with my book club. Phyllis and Bernie kept inviting me over to dinner or out to dinner with their friends, and my granddaughters were constantly stopping by to check up on me. I even took one of them on a cruise to the Caribbean a few years back. It was my first vacation without Joe, but we had never been to the Caribbean while he was alive, so I figured I might as well get on with the business of living for the both of us.

When I lie down at night, sometimes I can still feel his presence, and it's at these moments that I know he's still with me in spirit, if not in the flesh. I just have to keep remembering this as I decide on which car to buy today. Hell, I didn't even realize I was tearing up until Rosalie asked me if everything was all right. I reassured her, as I took out a tissue from my purse, and explained that I was just taking a stroll down memory lane.

"Joe?" she asked.

"Yes, I was just thinking that I'm about to part with the last car Joe and I bought together. I'll be okay. Really, I will."

"You know, Esther," Rosalie said. "I think Joe would be so very proud of you. The way you've carried on without him. I know you were never the type to fall apart without a man in your life, but still, it's quite an adjustment to make."

"I suppose he would be proud of me. But let's face it, he didn't marry me because of my deference to him," I said, my eyes still swelling with tears.

"Tell me about it, dear. You're a slightly softer and more palatable version of myself. Maybe that's why we've always gotten along so well, you and I."

"Truer words were never spoken, my dear," I responded, clutching her hand.

"Is everything okay back there?" Phyllis asked.

I told her not to worry, that I was just a little emotional today, and that I'd be all right in a few moments.

We decided to stop at the Cadillac dealership first since it was at the far end of town and then we would work our way backwards towards home. Upon entering, I looked around at the models on the showroom floor and was really underwhelmed by what I saw. I know I have to adjust my expectations as to what a Cadillac is supposed to look like, what with the downsizing craze that has taken over the car industry as a whole. But I wasn't seeing much that impressed me.

Well, there was this one Cadillac Fleetwood Coupe in blue with a matching half-vinyl roof that did catch my eye. It wasn't as stately as my '82 Deville, but it sure did look sharp. I opened the driver's door and got in behind the wheel. Now this is what luxury was supposed to be about! Button-tufted matching blue leather upholstery and glossy straight-grained wood trim that was made of actual real wood, according to the salesperson who had just walked up to the car.

"Ma'am," he said in a southern drawl. "Allow me to introduce myself. I'm Jefferson Beauregard Jackson, and I'm the proud owner of our little dealership. Moved up here from Mobile about twenty years ago. Built up this dealership from two sticks and a bit of good luck."

"Listen, mister," I responded curtly. "I've been buying Cadillacs from this dealership for years, so I'm well aware that what you just spewed out is a bunch of, oh how do you say it down there, a bunch of hooey."

"Well, ma'am, umm," he stuttered.

"Leave my presence now, and no one will get hurt," I advised. He made a beeline for the offices.

I took a few more moments reveling in the luxuriousness of this Caddy, but soon enough, Phyllis and the others came over to rain on my parade. They had another salesperson in tow.

"Mom," Phyllis started, "it's a beautiful car, but don't you think it's still too large of a vehicle for you to manage? Nancy here would love to show you the Eldorado or perhaps the Seville."

"Absolutely," Nancy interjected. "Why, the Eldorado and Seville are styled and sized with the modern 1980s woman of distinction in mind, and even though I know we have just met, I can tell that you are a woman of distinction."

Nancy was lying to me, just like Jefferson was, but at least her lies were very complimentary towards me. So, I gave her a pass and let her show me these two miniature Cadillacs on the showroom floor. I sat in the Eldorado, but it just didn't have the panache of that beautiful Fleetwood over there. And the Seville is really just a four-door version of the Eldorado, so I decided against inspecting it further.

"Phyllis," I said, turning to her. "I just don't know about this. This Eldorado is so small, and it feels so cramped inside. Plus, you can't even get it with a bench seat. It's bucket seats or no seats."

"Well, okay, Mom. Perhaps we should move on to another dealership then. There's nothing else that Cadillac has to offer that isn't either too large or too small. So we might as well hit the road."

"My apologies, Nancy," I said. "But these little mini Caddies just won't do. Thank you for your time."

We walked out of the dealership and settled back into my land yacht, as my daughter called it. It might be big, but it sure is comfy.

"Where to next?" Bernie asked.

"Let's try the Buick dealership. I haven't really kept up with their latest models, so maybe I'll be surprised and find something I like there," I responded.

"Oh, I saw a commercial the other night for that little two-seater they've started selling," Rosalie added. "I can't remember the name of it though. Senior moment, I suppose."

"You mean super senior moment," I teased.

"Careful, dear," she replied. "You're not that far behind me in age."

Well, this was certainly true. Just a little over five years to be exact. But five years might as well be twenty when you're in our age bracket. Oh sure, we're living longer lives now than our parents and grandparents did, but it's a question of whether these years are good years. I know a number of women who've lived as long as Rosalie has at eighty-five and still enjoy their lives. But there's something about the five-year stretch from eighty-five to ninety that trips up a lot of people. Muriel is one of the few I know approaching ninety who still has most of her faculties in reasonable working order.

My own mother lived to be the exact age that I am now, but the last few years of her life were plagued with one illness or injury after another. To tell you the truth, I think it all started with a nasty fall she took leaving her house one morning. She stumbled down her porch steps and fell flat on her face on the walkway. She managed to get herself up, but she was pretty shaken. A neighbor had seen her fall and came rushing to help.

I got a call later that afternoon from that neighbor telling me what had happened, so of course, I rushed right over. Leave it to my mother to take a spill and not tell me. She was an incredible woman, and I miss her dearly, but she definitely had a stubborn streak. Joe and I offered to have her move in with us after that fall, but she refused. What was her excuse, you wonder? Well, my mother told me that she had gotten in the habit of wearing nothing but her birthday suit around the house after my father died and didn't want the burden of having to wear clothes inside again.

I knew she was just pulling my leg, but I let it go. Unfortunately, the fall must have aggravated her arthritis because she slowly but steadily lost a lot of mobility. This led to another fall a year later, which put her in the hospital for a hip replacement. She never walked without a walker again. And when you're in your seventies and eighties, if you don't use it, you lose it.

So, her joints became even more arthritic, to the point where she really couldn't look after herself. Again, Joe and I offered for her to move in with us, but she still refused. She ended up moving in with her younger sister for a while, but her health continued to deteriorate. Finally, she moved in with my spinster sister, who took care of her until she passed.

I'm sure you see some parallels between my mother's refusal to move in with us and my refusal to move in with Phyllis and Bernie, but I've aged more gracefully than my mother did. And I hope to remain independent for as long as I can. But even I have to admit that I'm not where I was ten years ago. My ability to judge distances has clearly diminished. Just ask those poor mailboxes I've decapitated, if you don't believe me. I had always assumed Joe and I would grow old together, and then if necessary, move into a facility together. But I suppose it's time for me to really think about how I want to spend my remaining years.

There are so many things to consider, and taking care of Sarah these last few days has brought it all to the forefront of my mind. We are not promised that tomorrow will be as good as today is. Well, for that matter, we're not promised tomorrow period. But what I'm getting at is that I never really sat down and came up with a plan for my care when I reach the point of no longer being able to look after myself. And I'm nearly eighty! It seems as though I just spent the last five years learning how to live without Joe, and now I'm facing the reality that I will soon need to learn anew again. Hopefully not too soon, though.

I do have enough money to hire a home caregiver, a real one. Not like Muriel and me. We're just trying to help David and Dianne out in a pinch. But would a home caregiver be the right choice for me? I assume that by the time I need one, my ability to socialize and stay in contact with those I love will be greatly diminished, and I would be leading a very circumscribed life.

Of course, I could move into a facility on my own, and there would certainly be plenty of other elderly people to interact with. I have a friend who moved into one last year after she was having trouble managing the maintenance and upkeep on her house. Once or twice a month I go over and visit with her, and all she does is complain about the food. I told her it couldn't be that bad, so she had me taste her omelet one day. Well, let me tell you, it was barely edible. It was a frozen omelet that had been reheated. Oh, and the desserts there consist mostly of different types of canned fruit. Once in a blue moon, she gets a tiny piece of cake, but that's her only respite.

"Esther, dear," Rosalie began, breaking my train of thought. "Is everything all right?"

"Oh, I was just thinking about the future," I said.

"Don't bother. For us old birds, there's nothing to like about the future. Live in the present. Speaking of which, we're here at the Buick dealership."

And so we were. I realized we were surrounded by a ton of Buicks in all shapes and colors. We all got out of my car and made our way to the entrance, where a courteous salesperson opened the door for us.

10

The salesperson, whose name was Randy, asked us if there was anything he could help us with, but I told him we'd come find him when we were ready. I wanted to walk around the showroom first on my own. I told the others to stay put while I went and walked around the various models on the floor, and while I didn't notice any car that really wowed me initially, I was pleasantly surprised when I reached the far corner of the room.

What stood before me was a beautiful coupe in a striking copper color. The car had a long, sloping hood that ended in a neat and tidy setup of flush-mounted headlamps and an upward-pointed waterfall grille. Nice chrome moldings on the bumper and sides, and a wedge-shaped trunk with large split taillights separated by the license plate bracket. I got a little closer so I could read the model name and discovered that this was a Regal Coupe. I was in love with it!

That is, until I opened the driver door and sat inside. The seats were done in a tan mouse-fur-type cloth, not my favorite. The dashboard had a bit of a poor-man's space-age theme to it, with a full-length narrow pod that housed the gauges and not much else. Seemed like a waste of space to me. The radio and manual climate controls looked confusing to me, and the faux wood trim looked like cabinet liner material. I had gotten used to automatic climate control and wasn't sure I wanted to take a step backwards.

But when I got back out of the car and looked at the list price, my feelings softened somewhat as the car cost a whole lot less than what I was used to spending. I thought to myself, do I really want to invest a lot of money in a vehicle at this stage in my life? Especially given my penchant for running into mailboxes? I don't do long drives anymore, and I rarely get on the freeway unless absolutely necessary. It seemed like maybe this car would fit the bill for what I really needed versus what I really wanted.

I summoned the others over to see what I had found and to get their reactions.

"Oh, Mom," Phyllis started. "I love it! And what a beautiful color, too!"

"Seems a little too racy for you," Bernie added.

"It sure is a pretty car," Rosalie chimed in. "But come, let me show you what I found!"

Rosalie led us all to the front of the showroom where she pointed in excitement at a little white car. Ugh, mini Cadillacs and now mini Buicks.

"This," she said. "This is the car I saw on television that I was telling you about. They call it the Reatta, and it's a two-seat sporty car. I sat inside of it, and it has a touch screen for the main controls! I didn't even realize cars had this feature now!"

"Oh, but they do," Randy said as he walked up behind us. This car has a state-of-the-art heat-sensitive touch screen that

The Enlightenment of Esther

controls the radio, climate, trip computer, and maintenance diagnostics controls. She's a real beaut!"

"Um, Randy, is it?" I asked.

"Yes, ma'am."

"Why don't you take Rosalie here on a test drive of this little car that she's clearly fallen in love with?" I asked. "We'll wait here and do a little more browsing."

Before I could utter another word, Randy went to get the keys for the demo model, and he and Rosalie headed out the door for the test drive. I figured with her out of the way, I could have a serious conversation with Phyllis and Bernie and decide what to do. I absolutely loved the copper color of that Regal over there, but I wasn't sure I was in love enough with the entire car to purchase it.

"So, Mom," Phyllis began, "how about that Regal? Thinking of buying it?"

"Well, dear," I replied, "I think I would need to test drive it first. But I do like the color, and the price is more than reasonable. I'm not sold on the interior though. You can tell it's definitely not a Cadillac or even a mini Cadillac."

Bernie laughed, and Phyllis gave him a stern look. Clearly, Phyllis wanted me to buy the Regal and be done with it. But this could be the last car I buy, and I wanted to make sure I chose wisely. Everything else on the showroom floor was either too small, too large, or too boxy for my tastes. So it was either the Regal or move on to another car dealership.

A few moments later, Rosalie and Randy walked back in and informed us that she was going to buy the Reatta today, right now. Never mind the fact that she didn't have her car here to trade in. When I asked her about that, she said she'd sell it on her own. Gotta love Rosalie the Riveter! Once she makes up her mind to do something, there's no talking her out of it. So, we said our good-byes for the day, and I motioned to Phyllis and Bernie to follow me out the door. Phyllis looked like she was heartbroken.

We got back into my car, and Bernie asked me where I wanted to go next. I had thought about the Chrysler dealership, but then I remembered the commercial I had seen for Saab on the television last night. So I suggested we go there next.

"A Saab?" Bernie asked incredulously.

"Yes, I saw this commercial last night, and I figured, why not go and check out what Saab has to offer? At least it's not a Benz," I teased.

"Mom," Phyllis said, "I can't believe you're actually willing to consider a Saab. It's so, well, it's just so unlike you. I really thought we'd be burying you in a Cadillac. And now you're talking Saabs?"

"I just want to go see one in person. Look, if I don't like the Saabs, I promise you we can go back to the Buick dealership for a test drive of that Regal you're so desperate to get me into. Does this meet with your satisfaction?"

"Yes, of course, Mom. I just want you to be happy with whatever you decide on," Phyllis responded.

So, off to the Saab dealership we went. When we arrived, we got out of the car and walked in the door. A handsome salesperson with a buzz cut and a tan introduced himself as Pete and asked if there was anything he could help us with. I told him we were just browsing around and would come find him when we were ready.

Well, right in the center of the showroom was this absolutely stunning convertible. You know, I hadn't even considered a convertible. They seem so impractical in Ohio during the cold winters. A friend of mine had a Mustang convertible years ago, and she was always freezing inside of it when the temperature dropped below fifty degrees. But this convertible in front of me sure was strikingly good-looking.

"Oh, Pete!" I yelled. "We're ready for you now!"

"Glad to be of service," he said, walking over to us.

"Tell me about this car," I instructed, pointing to the convertible.

"This is our 900 Turbo Convertible. We call the exterior color Talladega Red, and it comes with a black power soft top. The seats are done in a tan color, the dash is black, and this particular one has the optional leather upholstery. It's definitely a very sharp-looking car. Here, let me open the driver's door for you so you can get in. Get the feel for the car."

At his direction, I sat behind the wheel and looked around. All I can say is that it sure wasn't a Cadillac, or even a Buick, but there was a certain charm to its simplicity. All of the controls were mounted high on the dash, and the gauges were very easy to read. The seats were very comfortable, and it looked like the backseat was pretty roomy for a two-door car. I went looking for the power seat adjustment buttons, only to find that there were none. This was a manual seat. Damn.

Well, I guess you can't have it all when you're looking at something this avant-garde. A power seat would be nice, but I suppose it's not a necessity. Same goes for automatic climate control, which this car was also lacking. At the same time, though, this car reminded me so much of what it was like to drive a car without all of the modern accessories I've so become accustomed to. There was a certain charm to it that I couldn't help but like, and I was absolutely tickled at the ignition located on the floor console. What a novel idea to keep your keys from dangling and banging into your knees.

"Now, Pete," I said. "How do these cars do in cold weather?"

"I'm glad you asked," he replied. "First, this car is front-wheel drive, rather than the rear-wheel-drive Cadillac you pulled up in. Front-wheel drive makes the car more stable during winter weather driving. The car also has heated seats and an electric rear windshield defroster built into the soft top."

"Speaking of soft tops," I said. "How does the material hold up? I mean, am I going to freeze my ass off in this thing?"

Pete was a little taken aback by my choice of words, and Phyllis visibly cringed. But I figured there was no point in beating around the bush. I mean, why bother even test-driving the car if it was going to leave me with icicles hanging down from my ears in the winter?

"Ma'am," he responded, "the top is insulated with triple lining, so you'll be as snug as a bug in a rug. Saab is a Swedish company, and the winters get pretty cold up there, from what I understand. All of their cars are made to be driven year-round, including this convertible."

"Call me Esther," I said. "And this is my daughter and son-in-law, Phyllis and Bernie."

"A pleasure to meet all of you. May I ask, what do you all drive?"

I told him that the Cadillac out front was mine, and that Phyllis and Bernie drove a Volvo and a Mercedes-Benz, respectively. He started making small talk with Bernie about the Benz, but I think he was really just trying to net another sale. I could have told him he was wasting his time since Bernie was in love with the Benz, but since he didn't ask me, I kept my mouth shut.

"Pete," I said, after sitting in the car long enough to get a feel for it, "I think it's time for a test drive. Do you have one available to test out?"

"Sure, Esther. Actually, we can take this one out if you'd like. I'll just go grab the keys and pull it out of the showroom. I'll meet you all out front."

The three of us exited to the front of the building while Pete went to pull the car out of the showroom and around to us. Phyllis proceeded to ask me where her mother was and what had I done with her. Bernie had this little smile on his face, clearly amused that I was even considering buying a Saab.

What I realized, though, was that I wasn't getting any younger, and I might as well live whatever years I have left to their fullest. And the idea of buying and driving around in a convertible seemed like a good start to really living. My Cadillac served me faithfully for many years, but I was starting to feel like it was a symbol of a life I no longer really had. I needed to start thinking of myself as a single working girl again, instead of just teasing myself about it.

Maybe I could even convince Muriel to go bar hopping with me after work one day! We'd pull up in my Talladega Red Saab convertible, and I bet you heads would spin. Well, at least until they realized that we were very elderly working girls and that our version of bar hopping would probably be more akin to bar shuffling.

The more I was musing about what life might have in store, the more I was talking myself into buying the Saab after the test drive. Car shopping really is exhausting, and I wasn't sure I wanted to face defeat and return to the Buick dealership to purchase the Regal. I was ready to be done and to get everyone off my back about needing to adjust to my age and downsizing my set of wheels.

Pete drove around with the Saab and got out. Even though it was a brisk fall day, he kept the top down, and I figured, why not? He motioned for me to get behind the wheel and for Bernie and Phyllis to make themselves comfortable in the rear seats. I asked Pete where we should drive to, figuring he probably already had a planned route, but he surprised me and said the sky's the limit, pointing upwards.

So I put the car in drive, and off we went!

I drove us on to I-270, the loop that runs around Columbus, and if I could have gotten away with it, I would have driven the whole loop. But after about ten minutes, Pete asked me if I was planning on turning around anytime soon. So, I exited the loop, turned around on a side street, and headed back towards the dealership.

It was at that precise moment of realizing I didn't want the drive to end that I decided to purchase the car. But I didn't want to lay all of my cards down on the table just yet. I wanted to make sure that I paid a fair price for both parties. I wasn't one to nickel-and-dime someone, but neither did I want to be taken advantage of.

After we walked back in to the dealership, we all sat down around Pete's desk and started crunching the numbers. He had someone else take a quick look at my Cadillac to determine what they would offer me as a trade-in. While my car was being inspected, Pete and I negotiated what I thought was a reasonably fair purchase price for the convertible. I didn't want to make it obvious that I was also looking for Bernie and Phyllis's approval, so I just stared at them out of the corner of my eye to see how they were reacting to the negotiations. Surprisingly, they didn't seem to have any visible objections.

When the valuation on my Cadillac came back at what I considered to be a fair number, I told Pete I was ready to sign on the dotted line. He asked me if I would be financing any part of the purchase, to which I said no. He then asked me if I wanted to keep my license plate or get a new one. I told him, "New life, new car, new license plate, please."

It took us about a half hour to get out of the dealership with my new car, but once we did, I was positively giddy! I drove us back to my place, and Phyllis and Bernie took off back to their house, still in shock over what I had just done. Hell, I still can't believe it myself! I bought a Saab! And not just any Saab, but a Saab 900 Turbo convertible in Talladega Red!

11

The rest of the weekend pretty much flew by. I drove all around town, showing the car off to anyone and everyone I could. Rosalie gave me a stiff smile, probably annoyed that I had stolen some of the thunder from her own new car purchase. Muriel was beside herself with joy when I pulled up in front of her house on Sunday and honked the horn for her to come out and see.

But my fun ended Monday morning when I remembered that I had promised Muriel I'd drive her over to her late husband's son's house for what was sure to be a heated confrontation. I called Muriel up to ask her what time she wanted to go. Can you believe she actually tried to back out of it? The nerve! Well, I suppose there was a part of me that wanted to let the whole thing go as well, but I just couldn't. It angered me to no end that this person was taking advantage of my dear friend, and I was bound and determined to put a stop to it.

"Muriel," I said, "we're going. No excuses. No delays."

"But," she started.

"No buts either," I said in response.

Muriel resigned herself to my insistence that we go and said to pick her up around noon. She said she needed some time to work her nerves up to the task. I told her I would pick her up at noon sharp. And, much to her disappointment, I had to let her know that we would have to ride with the top up since it was supposed to rain today.

You know, no one ever thinks about the downsides to having a convertible. In addition to not being able to enjoy it when the weather is uncooperative, the soft top creates some pretty big blind spots. I've adjusted my mirrors as best as I can, but the rest I'll just have to leave in God's hands. If he wants me to be safe, then he'll make it so. If he wants me to have an accident, then there's really nothing I can do. I was starting to have a real appreciation for preordination. It absolves me of any real responsibility for my actions!

I called Rosalie up and asked her if she wanted to tag along for the ride, figuring that three elderly women against one middle-aged man were better odds than two elderly women against one middle-aged man. But, predictably, she declined. She said that I ought not to be inserting my nose where it doesn't belong and that she wanted no part in what was about to happen. I criticized her for not wanting to help out a friend in need, and she criticized me for being too generous and kindhearted for my own good. We agreed to disagree.

When I pulled up to Muriel's house, she was already waiting for me on the front porch. But she just kept sitting there on her rocker. I got out of the car and went up to see why she hadn't moved. Her eyes were closed. At first, I couldn't tell if she was breathing or not, so I took my compact out of my purse and held the mirror side underneath her nose. Sure enough, it started fogging up, so I knew she was still alive. My guess is she got herself so worked up over this whole ordeal that she knew if she didn't wait outside, there was no way I'd be able to get her to take care of this extortion business.

So, I nudged her awake as gently as I could. It took a bit of coaxing, but she finally roused, said she was a little groggy, and asked me if we could postpone our trip. I told her in no uncertain terms that we were going, even if I have to carry her to the car myself.

Muriel slowly rose, an expression of resignation on her face, and we got into my beautiful new Saab. I asked her for the address, which I probably should have gotten from her earlier, but thankfully it was on a street I knew, just on the other side of downtown Columbus. It'd probably take us twenty minutes to get there. They say you can get anywhere in the Columbus metropolitan area within a twenty-minute drive, and as I've lived here all my life, I have found that to be true.

About halfway there, Muriel started to have a panic attack. She was practically hyperventilating, and I had to pull the car over and calm her down. I probably should have predicted this, and if I had, I would have stowed a brown paper bag in the glove box for her to breathe into. But I didn't, so all I had at my disposal were my calming words and reassurances that this was going to turn out okay.

I ran into a local donut shop and asked for a cup of water to bring to Muriel. Well, they said, no purchase no water. So, what was I to do but order a couple of donuts for us and pray that the sugar rush would give Muriel the boost in confidence to do what needed to be done? I ordered two maple-frosted donuts, two chocolate-frosted donuts, and two regular Cokes. I figured the more sugar we got into our systems the better. Neither one of us is diabetic, at least as far as I know.

Muriel was still looking a bit frantic when I got back in the car and handed her the donuts and the pop. Thankfully, the aroma of the donuts seemed to have a tranquilizing effect on her, and she started devouring them. She ate her two and then one of mine as well! I think next time I'll just bring a couple of sugar packets with me and empty them directly into her quivering mouth. It would have been cheaper.

After we finished off the donuts and the pop, a thought had occurred to me. I didn't even ask Muriel if her late husband's son works during the day. I mean, here we are trekking over to his house, and he might not even be home. I asked her then if she knew what his current employment status was, to which she said she didn't know and hadn't thought to ask. So, I told her we might as well go over and check. If he's home, we can do what we came here to do, and if not, we'll try back at another time, or maybe next weekend.

We arrived at the address that Muriel had for him, but we both decided we needed a few minutes to collect ourselves. It was one thing to plan such an attack. It was another thing entirely to follow through on it.

"Okay, Muriel," I started. "It's time to shit or get off the pot."

"Esther," she replied, "I'm surprised at you, using such language."

"Why? I say 'shit' all the time in my head. So, I figure, what's the difference if I just say it out loud? Driving this car has liberated me! I feel like a new woman—well, a new old woman anyway."

"Ugh, well, let's get this over with before I completely lose my nerve," Muriel responded.

So that's what we did. We got out of the car and walked up to a nicely maintained Tudor-style home with a very ornate, though out-of-place, wooden front door. Well, here goes. I rang the doorbell and waited for someone to answer. When no one came to the door, I rang the bell again. When still no one answered, I knocked on the door as loudly as my arthritic knuckles would allow.

We waited another minute and were just about to turn around when a voice from inside asked who it was.

"It's Muriel," she said with all the volume she could muster.

The door swung open, and to my utter surprise, Pete from the Saab dealership was standing before us, shirtless and with a towel wrapped around his waist. Under more pleasant circumstances, I'm sure Muriel's eyes would have started glazing over again. I knew Pete was handsome, but I didn't realize what great shape he was in!

"Pete!" I said, in total surprise.

"Wait," Muriel chimed in. "You know him?"

"Why, yes, I do. He sold me that beautiful car sitting out there on the street," I said, pointing to my new prized possession.

"Well," Muriel continued. "This is also Peter, my late husband's illegitimate son."

"But, wait," I said. "You told me he was biracial."

"Well, he is. Can't you tell just by looking at him?"

Needless to say, Pete was a bit confused and was clearly starting to get a bit irritated, I could tell. Just imagine opening your front door, wearing nothing but a towel, to find two elderly women arguing over whether you're biracial or not.

"Muriel, dear, you really need to do something about your eyesight. He's not biracial. He's just tan and has a buzz cut so you don't know what his hair actually looks like," I chided.

"Well, he looks biracial to me," Muriel responded.

If I were a southerner, I think this would be an opportune time to say something like "Bless your heart," but since I'm not,

I settled for a condescending stare and told her to ask him if he was indeed biracial. She did.

"No, ma'am," Pete responded. "If I were to take this towel off, you'd see just how white I really am."

Muriel was mortified with embarrassment, but I couldn't help but chuckle a little.

By this point, I was really at a loss for words. This was totally unexpected, that Peter and Pete would end up being the same person. Well, okay, maybe the thought should have crossed my mind when I bought the car, but since I was under the mistaken impression that Peter was biracial and Pete was clearly not to my eyes, I just didn't put the two together. But here we are, and the money-grubbing extortionist whom Muriel had described to me was nothing like the man I got to know as he sold me my Saab. Then again, I started to wonder if I really knew him at all.

I guess what I'm saying is that I really do feel he treated me fairly when I bought the car. So how could this seemingly fair salesman be the same person who is blackmailing Muriel now? Something just wasn't adding up, and I was determined as ever to get to the bottom of this. There's got to be an explanation, a missing piece of the puzzle.

"All right, Pete," I said. "We have some things that we need to discuss with you. But, if you wouldn't mind, why don't you go put on some clothes? We'll wait out here for you, unless you'd like to invite us in."

"I'll be back in a jiffy," Pete said and closed the door behind him as he went to throw something on.

Muriel looked at me, and I could tell she wanted to just hightail it out of here before he returned. But I held my hand up and said we were going to take care of this business with the money right here and right now. We drove all the way over here, and we weren't going to go back empty-handed.

"But, Esther," Muriel said. "Don't you think I should be the one to say whether we stay or go? This is my problem, not yours."

"Dear," I responded. "I'm the one who drove us over here, and I'm the one who bought the donuts and pop. Don't bite the hand that feeds and drives you, dear."

Muriel looked resigned to the miserable experience this was going to be for her. In case you haven't noticed, confrontation isn't her strong suit. And while I may not be as combative as Rosalie usually is, I can still hold my own when I need to. Pete was going to get a piece of my mind whether he liked it or not. I was counting on not.

You know, I was starting to feel a little shaky, though. Maybe all of that sugar I ingested was finally hitting my system with a wallop. I was going to have to figure out how to get Pete to invite us in to sit down. But just then the door opened again, and I had to think quickly.

"All right, ladies," Pete began. "Not that I don't have an idea of why you're here, but please, go ahead."

"Umm, Pete," I responded. "Muriel is feeling a bit faint. May we come in and have a seat to discuss what we came here to say to you?"

"I'm not feeling faint," Muriel unhelpfully added.

"Yes, you are," I replied.

"No, I'm perfectly fine," she said.

"No, you are not fine. You are feeling faint. We've known each other a long time, and I can tell just by looking at you that you are feeling faint," I responded, with a glaring expression on my face.

"Oh, yes, right. I'm feeling lightheaded all of a sudden," she said, her hand reaching towards her forehead in a grand gesture that was anything but authentic.

    I suppose I need to find a better acting partner the next time I decide to try to pull one over on some unsuspecting poor soul. Pete had a very skeptical look on his face and clearly didn't want to invite us in. But I suppose better manners prevailed, and he stood back to let us into his home.

12

We walked into Pete's house, Muriel on my arm trying to keep up the ruse of feeling faint. There was a dining room on the left and a living room on the right. The kitchen was straight ahead, and off of the kitchen to the right, there was a cozy family room with two overstuffed blue velour sofas, a wooden coffee table, and a brick masonry fireplace with a brass insert. The carpeting was beige, but in bad need of replacing. Brown wood crown moldings and chair rails completed the décor.

Oh, and there was an older woman sitting on one of the sofas. I wasn't sure whether she was part of the décor or not, but I figured she was worth mentioning. I'd hate for you to accuse me of not giving a complete picture of the environment in which Muriel and I found ourselves.

"Mother," Pete said to the older woman. "This is Muriel Schwartz and Esther Kellerman. They've come to pay us a visit."

Well, the woman just looked at us, and I wasn't sure if she was registering the reality that she had just come face-to-face

The Enlightenment of Esther

with Muriel, the wife of the man she had had an affair with fifty years ago—the affair that produced Pete. She was looking at me pretty intently though. It was a bit unnerving, I have to say.

I was about to address her, but I didn't know what her name was, so I asked Pete. He told us to address her as Mrs. Matthews.

"Mrs. Matthews," I said, extending my hand. "It's a pleasure to meet you. We've heard so much about you, dear."

But apparently, we indeed hadn't heard enough, because Pete informed us that she had had a stroke a number of years ago which made it very difficult for her to speak. I felt badly for her, but I didn't want to appear too sympathetic for Muriel's sake. I didn't want to visibly take pity on the woman who had had an affair with her husband.

"Mother can still understand everything that we say but is barely able to speak. And her motor skills are pretty diminished as well. With help, she can walk with a walker, but it's not safe for her to be alone."

"Well, who looks after her when you're at work? For example, when you sold me my car this past Saturday?" I asked.

"I have a home helper come in. My mother had been living in a nice facility up until a few years ago, but our financial situation changed, and we could no longer afford for her to stay there. What facilities we could afford were pretty run down, so she came to live with me instead."

I was beginning to see the bigger picture here. But I wanted Pete to explain further rather than me making assumptions that might or might not be true.

"Pete," I said. "Perhaps we should go into the other room and discuss what we came here to talk about. I'm not sure this is anything your mother needs to hear about, given her fragile state."

Pete agreed to this, and we all headed back towards the living room. I sat down in a floral-print armchair, and Muriel took a seat in a mauve-colored chair. Pete sat on the plaid sofa that was situated between our two chairs and behind a glass-top coffee table with an ornate brass base. There was an Aubusson rug underneath the table, as the floor in this room was made of parquet.

Has parquet gone out of style yet? I've never been a big fan of the stuff. I had a friend who literally believed in the "step on a crack and break your mother's back" superstition. She couldn't even enter a room with parquet flooring as a result. I kid you not.

"Mrs. Schwartz," Pete began, speaking to Muriel. "There are some things you may not understand or be aware of. And I hate to have to be the one to tell you, but you need to know."

Now why is it that there's always some sort of unexpected twist? I just wanted to come here to tell Pete that Muriel would no longer be sending him any more money, period. I didn't see why there needed to be a discussion, but it would seem that Pete had other plans.

You see, I had thought that if Muriel and I sat at opposite ends of the room, we could go at him from different directions if he became combative. He'd be shaking his head back and forth like he was watching a Ping-Pong match. But now I recognize the folly in my thinking. I could tell Pete was about to lay a big old egg in front of us, and I had wished we were both sitting on the couch together, arm in arm, to catch the damned thing.

I looked over at Muriel and noticed she was clutching the arms of her chair, her knuckles white with tension. Not that my knuckles were fairing much better, mind you. This, whatever it is he needs to tell us, is not going to go over well, but Muriel finally told him to proceed.

"Your husband, Morty," Pete said. "He was more than just an affair with my mother. He loved her. Oh, he loved you and your daughters dearly, but he loved my mother too. I'm sorry if it hurts you to hear this. That is not my intention."

"Then why? Why tell me this?" Muriel asked.

"Because it's the reason he kept sending money, even after I had grown up," Pete replied.

"I'm not sure I'm following," I interjected.

Pete explained that Morty had wanted to provide for them both as best as he could. Morty felt such guilt over not being able to really be there for the two of them the way a partner and father should. The money allowed Pete's mother to only have to work a part-time job so that she could be at home with Pete when he wasn't in school.

About twenty years ago, Pete's mother had had her stroke, and the money that Morty kept sending was used to help cover the costs of her healthcare needs. Pete had made up the difference, and was easily able to since he had been a high-powered investment banker before the stock market crashed two years ago.

Out of a job, he landed at the Saab dealership and went looking for Muriel to ask her why the checks had stopped coming in from Morty. It sounds like things had gotten pretty desperate for the two of them. So, Pete admitted to blackmailing Muriel into continuing the payments so that he could see to his mother's needs. Needless to say, he wasn't making nearly as much as a car salesman as he had been as an investment banker.

While I can't say that I approve of his blackmailing Muriel, at least I had a better understanding of why he did it. He clearly loved his mother deeply and wanted to do right by her. It's just a shame that it meant doing wrong by Muriel.

"Pete," I said, "there's something that I don't understand. Why are you still working at the Saab dealership? I mean, I'm sure by now some of those banking jobs have come back. You'd be able to take care of your mother without extorting money from my dear friend. And I would so appreciate it if you could find a way to, you know, stop the extortion."

"Well to be honest, Mrs. Kellerman," he responded. "The Saab dealership is much less stressful than the job I had as an investment banker. Plus, having my mother around has been a surprisingly pleasant experience. When she lived at the facility, I'd see her maybe once a week. Now I get to see her every day, and the dealership has been really good about working with me regarding my schedule should the home health worker have to cancel at the last minute."

This last part made me even prouder of my new purchase, knowing that my money was going to a reputable company that cared about its employees. I deliberately waited a beat before responding, hoping that Muriel would begin to explain her current financial situation to him. But I suppose I should have known better. Why should she do the dirty work when she has me here to do it for her?

"We need to talk about the money," I said.

"Yes, I figured that's why you both were here. I was surprised to see you, Mrs. Kellerman. I had no idea you knew Mrs. Schwartz," he responded.

"Surprise, surprise!" I added. "Look, Pete, the short version of this story goes like this. Muriel cannot afford to keep sending you money, even if the money is being used for a somewhat noble cause. She understands and is willing to accept the consequences of your outing her late husband as a philanderer."

"No, I'm not," Muriel piped in.

"Yes, Muriel, you are," I snapped.

"I don't think I can bear it," she replied.

"Well, it's either that or sell your house and move in with one of your daughters. But eventually, when you pass on, your daughters are going to go through your finances. They will discover these payments, and they will have questions that you won't be here to answer. Have you thought about that?"

"Umm, no, Esther. I suppose not," Muriel admitted.

"Muriel has had to start working again, just to make these payments to you, Pete," I snapped at him. "She's working as a caregiver for an elderly neighbor who suffers from dementia. As I'm sure you can imagine just by looking at her, Muriel isn't capable of doing this on her own. So, guess who's helping her?"

My anger was boiling over now.

"You?" Pete asked.

"You got it!" I confirmed.

Pete had this look of amazement in his eyes, that two women in their twilight years would even consider taking care of an elderly neighbor with dementia. And then a devilish smile started to appear across his face, and I started to worry that we had walked into something we were totally unprepared to take on.

"Well, then," he audaciously began. "Since the two of you are already in the home healthcare business, how would you feel about taking on another patient?"

I just knew it. This was what he was angling for. A way to dump his mother on us. I mean, do we look like we're in any shape to take care of another elderly woman? Did someone spray-paint STUPID on our foreheads and forget to tell us?

"Peter," Muriel replied. "No."

"But think about it this way," he responded. "If I can find

someone to care for Mother for free, then you wouldn't have to keep paying me. That's where all the money goes, for her care."

"You've got a lot of nerve, Pete," I interceded. "Let's get one thing straight, right here and right now. Muriel isn't going to be paying you anymore. She can't afford it. Second, are you seriously asking Muriel to help care for the woman who had a years-long affair with her late husband? Have you no couth, or has the irony been completely lost on you?"

But before Pete could respond, his mother came into the room on her walker. I suppose our voices were carrying into the other room, even with a solid wall in between. Well, maybe the wall wasn't so solid. After all, I have no idea who constructed this house or to what standards it was built. I had half a mind to get up and see if I could punch my fist through the wall. That's how frustrated I was becoming of this whole situation.

Pete got up to help his mother, but she waved him away. She walked over to Muriel and grasped her right hand. With great difficulty, she managed two words: "I'm sorry."

Muriel, however, couldn't look her in the face. I don't know if Muriel was about to tear up herself, or if she was incensed by the gesture. Think about it. How would you react if the object of your spouse's affection had, under great duress, apologized to you? I know Muriel pretty well, but even I couldn't discern her reaction at this point.

Had Mrs. Matthews been able to speak with less effort, I'm sure her apology would have been a bit more, umm, comprehensive. I wonder if she had had any speech therapy after her stroke. I think it's common practice now for stroke victims, but twenty years ago, who knows? So I asked Pete, and he said they had tried to work with her to get as much of her speech back as possible. I then suggested that perhaps there have been advancements in speech therapy since his mother first had her stroke.

"Pete," I said, "I'm going to make you an offer purely out of the goodness of my heart."

Muriel was trying to get Mrs. Matthews to let go of her hand, with no success I might add.

"Oh?" he asked. "What did you have in mind?"

"First, I'm going to pay for a full medical workup for your mother to see if there's any potential for further improvement in her condition. Look, even the nicest of facilities have to prioritize the care that they give, and if your mother wasn't showing much improvement once she was settled in there, they probably weren't doing all that they could have done for her."

"I suppose it couldn't hurt to see what more can be done for her. But after all these years, do you really think there's any chance?"

Mrs. Matthews turned her gaze towards Pete, and without uttering a word she communicated that she wanted the workup.

"Second, if there's any hope for improvement, I will see to it that she gets the treatment and therapy that she needs. Third, I will be taking over the monthly payments that Muriel has been making that you've been using for your mother's care."

I could tell that Muriel didn't want to accept this charity from me, but I'll be damned if I'm going to watch her sell her house when she should be enjoying it for whatever time she has left. Pete seemed okay with the arrangement though.

"I have one condition," I continued. "You will commence looking for a new job back in the investment banking field that pays significantly better than what you're currently making at the Saab dealership. And when you do land such a job, you will take over the financial responsibilities associated with your mother's day-to-day care."

Pete looked a little defeated. I think he genuinely thought that I was going to basically give him a free ride to continue on without making any changes to his lifestyle. Oh, the nerve of him! He took a few moments to mull over this offer, but he finally agreed.

"Oh, also," I added, "should you need to interview for such a job, I will fill in as an emergency caregiver for your mother if you can't make other arrangements. You should know that my Tuesdays, Thursdays, and Fridays are currently booked. So, please try to schedule any interviews on Mondays or Wednesdays."

Pete agreed and was starting to show at least a modicum of gratitude for my generosity in trying to help him find a more workable situation for his mother's care.

"Oh, one more thing," I began to ask. "What's your mother's first name?"

"Lilia."

13

On the drive home, Pete's mother's name kept running through my mind. Lilia. Lilia was the name of Joe and Rosalie's sister who had died as a young woman. No one would ever talk about her, much less speak her name, so I barely even remembered it myself. The other sisters were all still alive. Two were living out in California, another had found her way to Oklahoma, and the youngest was in Las Vegas. Of the seven siblings, only Rosalie and Joe had remained in Ohio. Joe was the second oldest and would have been eighty-three if he were still with us. Lilia was the second youngest.

But Lilia Kellerman is dead, and Lilia Matthews is very much alive. I've never known any other Lilias, which probably explains why the name was stuck in my mind. Well, there was that one Lilia in *The Ten Commandments* movie who was in love with Joshua. But that's it as far as I can tell. It's a beautiful name for sure.

I dropped Muriel off and headed home, exhausted from our errand. I parked the car in the garage, walked into the house, and set my purse down on the kitchen table. I checked my answering machine and listened to a message left by David. He wanted to know if Muriel and I could stop by this evening for dinner. I suppose this was his way of wanting to thank us for stepping in and helping with Sarah's care.

David had left his office phone number in the message and asked for me to call him there, so I did. I told him that we appreciated the gesture, but that we had had a busy day and were not up to it. Okay, I probably should have run it by Muriel first, rather than speaking for the both of us, but I didn't want Muriel to think that we had to go just because we were invited. She needed the rest, and so did I since we'd both be back at David's tomorrow taking care of Sarah. I have a strict one-decrepit-old-lady-per-day policy, and seeing Sarah tonight would have made two. I know, that sounds a bit harsh, but hasn't anyone ever told you that surrounding yourself with the elderly can be depressing?

Anyway, I sat at the kitchen table, pondering what to do about Lilia. I knew I'd have to make some calls to get her in to the specialists that she would need to see, but more than that, there was something about meeting her that was unsettling to me—yet, I couldn't figure out what was bothering me about it. Maybe it was the way she was looking at me. Or maybe it was just all in this crazy head of mine. The phone rang, giving me a jump, so I went to answer it.

"Esther," Rosalie said.

"Hello, dear," I replied.

"How about you and me go to the club for dinner?" she asked.

"As long as you're driving, sure. I've had an exhausting day," I responded.

Yes, I realize I just turned down an invitation from David,

only to turn around and accept one from Rosalie. But I just felt like I wanted her company tonight and maybe even needed it. I had a lot on my mind and needed a good sounding board. And if there's anything I can count on, it's that Rosalie will always give me her unvarnished opinion.

"Great, I'll pick you up at six-fifteen. You'll get to ride in my new car!"

"I'm looking forward to it. See you then," I said as I hung up the phone.

I thought about asking Muriel if she wanted to join us, but then I remembered that Rosalie's new car only has two seats. Who ever heard of an eighty-five-year-old woman buying a two-seater?

A few hours later, Rosalie showed up right on time, and I walked out the front door to meet her. Even I had to admit her car looked pretty sharp, despite the fact that it could only seat two people. I had a hard time getting into the car, since it sat pretty low to the ground, but if you ever tell anyone, I'll deny it to my dying day. I just wondered how Rosalie was getting used to this car's height or lack thereof.

"Rosalie, dear," I began, "I meant to ask you, what did you do with your old car?"

She had a 1981 Chrysler Imperial that she had loved. But like my 1982 Cadillac, the car really was too big for her to manage. I remember the day she bought it, though. Joe and I had gone with her to the dealership, thinking she was going to buy a New Yorker, but then she saw this gleaming glacier-blue Imperial coupe sitting in the showroom. The salesperson told us it was a very exclusive Frank Sinatra edition, and that the color was chosen to match Sinatra's famous blue eyes. Well, all it took was Rosalie sliding into the matching glacier-blue leather seats, and she was sold on it right away. She always did have a thing for Ol' Blue Eyes.

"It's still parked in the driveway," Rosalie answered. "I'll probably take it to a used-car lot sometime this week and tell them to make me their best offer for it. The car is in practically new condition."

"Well, aside from the dent it sustained when you ran off your own driveway and into a fire hydrant," I teased. She was not amused.

As we drove on towards the club, Rosalie kept trying to show me all of the different things she could control from the touch screen, but I kept swatting her hand back towards the steering wheel. Every time she started to press the screen to demonstrate a function, the car would start to veer out of the lane. I reminded her that she's an eighty-five-year-old woman driving at night and that she really should just focus on the road ahead.

We pulled up to the front entrance of the club and waited for a valet attendant to come out to relieve us of the car. Of course, Rosalie insisted on going over the finer details of how to operate the touch screen just in case the attendant needed to access any of the controls. I thought to myself, what controls could he possibly need to fiddle with on the twenty-second drive it would take for him to park the car in the valet lot? But I kept my mouth shut.

After the car was dispensed with, we walked in to the club and were greeted by my favorite maître d', Walter. He's always so kind to us and considerate of our preferences for where in the dining room we like to sit. Yes, I know our membership dues pay his salary, so he pretty much has to be nice to us, but he really does go the extra mile.

We sat down at our favorite table and started looking over

the menu. All I really wanted was a scoop of their delicious raspberry chocolate chunk ice cream, but Rosalie would not have approved. I suppose Phyllis wouldn't have either if she were here. I really should have called Phyllis and Bernie and asked them to meet us here for dinner tonight. I don't know why I hadn't thought of doing so. It would have saved me from having to rehash everything that had happened earlier today for a second time.

When the waiter came, Rosalie ordered the meatloaf, and I ordered the roast chicken. The waiter asked us what we'd like to drink, and we both ordered glasses of white wine—a pinot grigio for me and a chardonnay for her. The waiter asked if we wanted some bread to tide us over until our meals were ready, but we declined. It was either bread or dessert for us, and we definitely both preferred dessert.

"So," I began as the waiter walked away to fetch our respective wine orders. "I had quite an eventful day. Against your advice, Muriel and I went over to Pete's house to confront him about his extorting her for money."

The expression on Rosalie's face soured a bit.

"I don't know why I even bother voicing my opinion to you, Esther. You never do as I suggest," she snapped.

"Be that as it may," I responded, brushing off her snippy attitude. "Let me start by saying that he's not biracial. Muriel's eyes are getting worse. He's just got a rich tan and buzzed haircut, but Muriel's eyes are clearly getting worse. She wouldn't believe me when I told her he wasn't biracial, so she asked him herself. Can you imagine actually asking someone if they were biracial?"

Rosalie chuckled.

"Anyway, I managed to get him to invite us inside by making Muriel pretend she was feeling faint. Oh, wait, that was after he came back to the door once he finished putting his clothes on."

"You mean he was in the nude?" Rosalie asked, not sure whether to ask for more details.

"No, silly. He had a towel wrapped around his waist. He must have been in the shower when we announced our presence on his doorstep. So, he lets us in and leads us into the family room where his mother was sitting."

"He lives with his mother," she mused.

"Yes, but it's not what you think. She suffered a stroke years ago, and when he lost his high-paying job not long ago, he couldn't afford to keep her in the facility where she was living. Oh, did I mention he sold me my Saab? I didn't realize that Peter and Pete were the same person, but apparently, they are. I think he was just as shocked to see me as I was to see him!"

Rosalie looked a little perplexed.

"So, he's taking care of his mother and working at the car dealership to make ends meet? Who looks after his mother when he's at work?"

"Ahh, I'm glad you asked. He hires a caretaker to come in and sit with her, much as Muriel and I are doing now for Sarah. And that's where Muriel's money comes in. He's been using it to pay the caregiver, and until a couple of years ago, to help out with the costs of the facility she was in."

"So how did you and Muriel leave things with him?" she asked.

"Well," I began with a slightly guilty look on my face. "I told him that I would take over Muriel's payments until he could get another job back in his former high-paying profession."

Rosalie shook her head.

"How predictable of you," she teased. "Everybody had

better watch out when Esther Kellerman gets her checkbook out."

"And, um, I agreed to pay for a medical specialist to do another evaluation on his mother. She had the stroke twenty years ago, but it seemed to me that whoever was overseeing her rehabilitation back then had just sort of given up on her. She's totally lucid. Of that I am sure. But she can barely get around on a walker, and her speech is terrible. With great effort, she apologized to Muriel for sleeping with her late husband."

"Is that it, or is there more? Just wondering if I should ask the waiter to bring over a whole bottle."

"Well, I also agreed to pay for any physical or speech therapy that might still be of benefit to her. And, I told Pete I'd look after his mother if he gets an interview on short notice and can't arrange for a caregiver."

Rosalie just shook her head in disapproval, but the waiter brought our glasses of wine, which seemed to lift her spirits a bit. She held back on ordering that whole bottle.

"Oh, and one more thing," I added, taking a big gulp of my wine. "His mother's name is Lilia."

14

Rosalie looked like she had just seen a ghost. She dropped her glass of chardonnay all over herself, and I had to signal to the waiter to come bring us some extra cloth napkins. Like me, she probably hadn't known too many Lilias during the course of her lifetime.

"Tell me about her," I said as Rosalie sopped up the mess she had made. "Tell me about your sister. No one in the family would ever talk about her. At least not to me. All I have is a rough guess of when she passed based on the timing of when Joe had said that you all had sat shiva for her. I had gotten the impression that she was never to be discussed."

Rosalie looked like she wanted to crawl out of her skin, anything to get away from having to discuss her deceased sister. I wondered what could possibly have happened to Lilia Kellerman that was so awful that her family refused and still refuses to speak of it.

Pulling herself together, Rosalie said, "I will not discuss losing her."

"Then tell me about her. Tell me what she was like. Tell me anything! She's been such a secret. Was she a kind person? Did she have any particular talents? What was her favorite food?"

"She was beautiful. Inside and out. You know I pretty much raised Lilia and our youngest sister. I never knew a sweeter soul," Rosalie said.

"Go on," I encouraged.

"Lilia would put on little plays for us every night. She loved to sing and dance. As she got older, she started dreaming of a life in Hollywood, but that was only after the old talkies came out. Lilia didn't think her talents would lend themselves well to silent pictures. And believe me, she could act. She would have given Vivian Leigh a run for her money if she had auditioned for the part of Scarlet."

"She sounds delightful," I offered.

"When the Depression hit and my husband lost his job, the debt collectors would start coming around. I would make Lilia answer the door. With her acting abilities, Lilia would convince them that we would have the money we owed very, very soon. And when some of those same debt collectors would come around for a second or third time, she'd launch into a rendition of Fannie Brice's 'My Man' and have them in a trance with her voice."

"Sounds like a powerful gift. Oh, how I wish I could have been a singer," I commended.

"Really, Esther?" Rosalie asked. "I never knew. I've sat next to you in synagogue for years, and I've never really thought you had much of a talent for singing."

"Well, I think that remark was a bit uncalled for, Rosalie," I snapped.

"Look, when the first digit in your age is an eight, then you've earned the right to speak your mind. You're not quite there yet, Esther. Almost, but not quite. Besides, they say you tease the ones you love."

"So I've heard. But anyway, what was Lilia like as a young woman? I mean, after she left your house."

"Esther, you know as well as I do that women didn't move out on their own back then. Oh, Lilia could have moved back in with our mother, but she didn't want to. She had this resentment towards our mother, because in her eyes, our mother abandoned her and dumped her onto my husband and me. Lilia never forgave her for that, and our mother went to her own grave full of regret as a result."

"Societal mores have certainly changed since we were young women ourselves, Rosalie. But tell me about her. Tell me what Lilia was like as woman, not just as your younger sister."

"Well, Lilia could light up a room just by entering it. Her long, beautiful, and naturally curly brown hair. Her iridescent green eyes that some would swear were the prettiest shade of blue they had ever seen. A figure I never could have hoped to match, even on my best day, and a radiant smile that could charm even the hardest of hearts."

"Sounds like I could have been her twin," I teased.

"Esther, dear, no," Rosalie responded. "Remember, it was only a year or two after she left us that you and Joe met. So, I knew you when you were not much older than she was at the time. You were a handsome woman for sure, but you were no Lilia."

"Well, that was uncalled for," I snapped again. "I might not have been a Greta Garbo, but I've been known to turn a head or two in my day."

"Oh, never mind," Rosalie replied. "Didn't mean to offend you, dear."

The Enlightenment of Esther

Returning the subject back to the topic at hand, I asked, "Did Lilia ever have any serious suitors?"

"My goodness, yes. She was usually less serious about them than they were of her, but there was one in particular. . . ." Rosalie trailed off.

I didn't know whether to prod Rosalie further. She seemed to have lost herself in thought, or perhaps in reminiscence. But I could tell by the look on her face that the memories she was reliving were upsetting her. I reached my hand across the table and grabbed hers, as I could see the tears starting to trickle down from her eyes onto her cheeks. I reached into my purse with my other hand and grabbed a tissue for her.

"I'm all right, really," she said in a weakened voice.

"Dear, you don't appear to be all right to me," I replied.

"No, I suppose not. I loved Lilia as if she were my own. Nearly sixty years later, I still have trouble talking about her."

I wanted to press Rosalie further, as it was clear she had some unresolved feelings over whatever had happened to Lilia, but our waiter had arrived with our food. I was certainly hungry, and I thought that maybe having a bite to eat would help Rosalie recover her composure. I dropped the subject for the time being and began to enjoy the food set before me by the Good Lord and by my membership dues.

As I was taking a bite of my roast chicken, a thought occurred to me. What could have happened to Lilia that Rosalie still won't talk about it, even all these years later? I know I've mentioned to you that she believes in being philosophical about death and the loss of loved ones, but there was nothing philosophical about the tears that were streaming down her cheeks just a moment ago. This loss, the loss of Lilia was particularly painful for her, even now. But I didn't know why.

Should I have just let it be? Probably so, but I wasn't known for just letting the cards lay where they had fallen. No, I wanted answers. She wasn't just Rosalie's sister. She was a sister-in-law of mine whom I never had the chance to know. What could have happened to this beautiful creature?

"Rosalie," I started to say as I finished off the chicken.

"No," she quickly replied. "I don't want to talk about it. I hope that wherever she is, she is at peace, and that someday soon I'll get to see her again."

I suppose I had to respect Rosalie's wishes, but it was absolutely killing me to do so. I just sighed and signaled to the waiter to come over so I could put my order in for some of that raspberry chocolate chunk ice cream I've been pining for all night. Rosalie ordered a piece of cheesecake for herself, and we both asked for some coffee. Regular for me, and decaf for her.

"Esther, dear," Rosalie began after we both started on our desserts a moment later. "There are some things that are just better left unsaid. But, if you'd like, why don't you drop by one day, and we can go through some old family photos I have. Photos you probably haven't seen, since Joe probably didn't have any copies of these. You can see Lilia for yourself."

"I'd like that," I said, determined not to press the issue further. "I've only seen one or two photos of her, ever."

"I would, too," she added.

We finished our coffee and desserts and headed back out towards the lobby area, saying a goodnight to Walter. Stepping out into the brisk fall night was surprisingly refreshing. Rosalie gave the ticket for her car to the valet, and within a minute we were heading off towards home in the two-seater Buick. This time, I decided to hold my hand over the touch screen so that she wouldn't be tempted to show me any more of the gadgets and gismos that this mini Buick contained. I really didn't want to end up in a ditch.

The Enlightenment of Esther

"Why don't you come in for a bit?" I asked as Rosalie pulled up to my house.

"Can't, got a hot late-night date to get ready for," she joked.

"Oh, yes, I forgot. You've got to get yourself all fixed up for Johnny Carson. He'll be very disappointed in you if you're not all gussied up for him," I teased.

"Shh, don't tell that new young wife of his," Rosalie chuckled. "But if you have to, just tell her he decided to go in a different direction. Older instead of younger."

I got out of Rosalie's car and headed back into my house for another late evening alone. I don't mind the quiet and solitude, but every once in a while, I just wish there was someone sitting next to me on the sofa to share a laugh with when watching television. Sometimes I actually find myself talking to myself. It's an eerie feeling, for sure.

I set my purse and keys down on the table, figuring I'd give Muriel a call to see how she was faring after our adventurous day. Picking up the receiver, I dialed her number. There was no answer, and she doesn't have an answering machine. I knew Muriel was tired out from today, but she doesn't usually go to bed this early. I looked at the clock on the oven, which read 8:30 p.m. She should still be awake.

Calling two more times and still getting no answer, I started to worry. I was so tired myself, but I decided to go over to Muriel's to check on her. Instead of getting in my car, I figured I'd just walk over there. It's a bit chilly outside, but not bone-chillingly cold. So, I put on a coat, changed my shoes, and walked the few blocks to her house.

When I got there, the lights were all still on, so I assumed she was still awake. But where was she, and why didn't she answer the phone? I walked up to the front door and rang the bell. No answer. I knocked on the door, and finally, I heard a murmur from inside. I yelled her name, but all I got was more murmuring. The blinds were all closed, so I couldn't really see inside. I had a key to her place, but I didn't have it on me, so I turned around and walked back to my house to retrieve it.

Upon my return after getting Muriel's key, I opened her front door and found nothing amiss. Well, except for Muriel. I didn't see her in any of the front rooms, so I made my way back to the family room in the rear left side of the house. And that's where I found Muriel. Gagged and tied.

"Oh my," I said, as they were the only words I could muster.

I immediately began working to loosen the gag around her mouth, and when I got it undone, the words just spilled out of her mouth.

"They were after something specific. Something they thought I had."

"Who?" I asked. "Who were they?"

"The robbers!" she fumed. "They were looking for some sort of safe deposit box key, but I told them that when Morty died, I turned everything that I had of his back over to the bank. They didn't believe me, so they searched the home from top to bottom. I asked them to untie me, and that's when they put the gag in."

"Of all the nerve," I exclaimed. "I'm calling the police, and then I'm calling Phyllis and Bernie to come over."

"Wait, Esther. Would you mind untying me before you make those calls?"

"Oh, right, sure," I said, not thinking clearly.

I started to untie Muriel from the chair she was trapped in, and as I was doing so, she explained to me that the robbers said the safe deposit box belonged jointly to Morty and to a Mr. Nat Levinson. She had no idea who this Mr. Levinson was, and neither did I. But according to the robbers, Mr. Levinson was in some financial trouble and needed access to the contents in that box.

I started to ask why Mr. Levinson didn't just use his key, but then I remembered that there's usually only one key given to the owners of the box. Something wasn't sitting right with me about this whole mess, but I decided to let the police handle the matter, just as soon as I could call for them. I was having trouble with these knots in the rope still binding Muriel's feet to the chair legs.

"Listen, Esther," Muriel began. "I hate to do this to you since you've been such a good friend to me, but do you think you might be able to handle Sarah tomorrow on your own? This whole ordeal has really shaken me."

"Yes, dear, I'll take care of Sarah. Maybe I can convince Phyllis to come over and help out a bit, just to give me a break or two. We'll take care of it. Never you worry."

I finally got the last of the ropes untied, called the police, and called Phyllis and Bernie to come over. Once the police were done taking their notes and the others had arrived, I took my leave, unsure if I'd even have the strength at this point to walk home. That's how tired I was feeling.

15

The next couple of weeks went by in a blur. I ended up taking care of Sarah without any help from Muriel that whole first week after the robbery. She said her nerves were too frayed to help out. I thought maybe I'd be on my own with Sarah for a day, not the entire rest of the week. I should have had that Wednesday off, but David and Dianne's other caregiver for Sarah had some sort of emergency. And since Phyllis told me she was too busy to come over and help out, I was stuck with Sarah for four days in a row.

I have to say, the experience gave me a real appreciation for those husbands and wives who end up taking care of their other halves through these long illnesses. Or my sister for that matter, who took care of our mother during her final years. It takes real love and dedication to so fully and completely devote yourself to the care of another. I can't say that I had any such dedication or love for Sarah, but I did for Muriel, which was the only reason I was helping in the first place.

The whole experience made me reevaluate how I felt about

Joe's sudden death. At the time, I remember feeling so cheated, cheated out of many more years I should have had with him. But when you really get down to it, death by a projectile object causing you to fall out of a gondola isn't so bad compared to the years-long battle with Dementia that Sarah was suffering from. When it's my time to go, I hope I go quickly and without a lot of fuss.

Oh, and the police never got anywhere in tracking down Muriel's robbers. And since neither one of us even knew who Nat Levinson was, we really had no way to do any amateur sleuthing ourselves, but believe you me, if we had had any kind of lead, we would have been on the case. We'd be like a pair of Jessica Fletchers.

Anyway, Muriel did come back the following week, which gave me a little more time to work on my other project, finding the right specialists to evaluate Lilia. This took some doing, and some calling in of favors, but I managed to get her in to see one of the best stroke specialists in the greater Columbus area. Pete was thrilled when I called to give him the details for her first appointment. I also suggested that he call the doctor to relay any pertinent information regarding his mother's health that I may not have been aware of. The appointment is for Wednesday, November 1st. Just two days from today.

I was sitting down to enjoy my morning cup of coffee and plan out my day when the phone rang.

"Hello?" I asked, after picking up the receiver.

"Mrs. Kellerman, it's Pete."

"Oh, hello there, Pete. To what do I owe the pleasure of your call?" I asked, laying it on a bit thick.

"Well, you're not going to believe this," he started. "But I managed to land an interview for a position as a financial advisor at a local investment firm."

"That's wonderful news!" I exclaimed.

"It is, but...."

"But what?" I asked, with a knowing sensation in the pit of my stomach.

"It's this Wednesday. You know, the same day as my mother's appointment with the stroke specialist you had arranged for her to see."

"Well, just tell them you have to reschedule. There, problem solved," I said as assertively as I could muster.

"Umm, I tried. I told the hiring manager that I have a family conflict, but he didn't seem to care. He said the interview would be Wednesday, or there would be no interview for me."

"Perhaps your mother's caregiver could take her then. I know it's not ideal and that you would rather be there yourself. Hell, I'd rather you be there too," I said.

"She can't. I asked."

"Oh, dear," I lamented, getting a clearer picture of where this was heading.

"Could you possibly find it in your heart to take her? In a way, it makes sense, since you're so generously paying for my mother's consultation in the first place."

"How about I go on your interview for you instead?" I asked, half joking, half serious.

"Believe me, Mrs. Kellerman. If that were a realistic possibility, I wouldn't hesitate to take you up on that offer."

"Oh, all right," I said, after a long pause. "If I must, I must. Anything to help you land a higher-paying job. I'll pick your mother up around ten on Wednesday. That'll give us plenty of time to get over to the stroke specialist."

"Thank you," he said, clearly relieved that I had solved yet another one of his problems.

I hung up the phone and just sat there, staring out the

The Enlightenment of Esther

window and wondering how I had gotten myself involved in another mess. I barely knew the woman and now I'm taking her to a serious medical appointment. Rosalie would have a field day with this if I told her about it, so I decided that for once, I'd just leave her in the dark.

There really wasn't much on my agenda today except for my hair appointment in the afternoon, so I leisurely read the morning paper and took my time showering and dressing. I watched a bit of television, fixed myself some lunch, and then waited until it was time to leave for the salon. Rosalie and I had the same hairdresser, and we both had appointments today, so I had told her I'd swing by and pick her up. No sense in us driving separately since our appointments were scheduled back to back.

I drove up to Rosalie's around one-thirty and honked the horn. She came out a few seconds later and planted herself into the passenger seat. She was wearing a beautiful turquoise blue sweater over a pair of black slacks. Very sharp, I must say. I, on the other hand, was wearing a loose-fitting buttoned blouse that I didn't care what happened to. I was getting my hair colored, so I needed to make sure whatever I was wearing could be thrown out if need be. Rosalie didn't have this problem since she had let her hair go gray many years ago. But before she did, she used to dye it jet black. I swear, she looked like someone had tried to lay asphalt on top of her head.

"So, I was thinking about having Thanksgiving dinner at my place this year," I said as we drove along to the salon.

"Oh?" she asked. "Why? I thought you were so relieved when Phyllis started taking over the holiday dinner responsibilities a few years ago."

"I was, but I think I'd like to host the dinner at least one more time while I still can," I replied.

"Esther, I know you too well. What have you got cooking up there in that head of yours? I know you've got some ulterior motive."

"Well, I'd like to invite some extra people this year, and I wouldn't feel right foisting extra mouths to feed onto Phyllis."

"And who did you have in mind?" she asked.

"For starters, Muriel. Her daughters and their families have decided to go to the Bahamas for a little vacation over the holiday, and she doesn't feel up to traveling."

"Uh-huh. Who else?" Rosalie pestered.

"Sarah, David, and Dianne," I responded. "They're still pretty new to the neighborhood, and given Sarah's condition, they're probably not getting much in the way of invitations. It'd be a shame for them to spend the holiday by themselves."

"Esther, dear. Did it occur to you that they might actually want to spend it by themselves? From what you've described, Sarah can be a handful. I think you're being foolhardy in even considering inviting them. If you do invite them, I might just stay home."

"Oh, really now. I wish you would untie that bonnet of yours and let that poor bee out. You're not going to stop me from extending a bit of kindness to them."

"Fine. Who else?" she asked, quite perturbed now.

"Well, I was thinking about asking Pete and Lilia to come, too."

"Have you lost your mind?" Rosalie fumed. "You barely know these people. And what would Muriel say? Do you really think she'd want to break bread with the woman who had a years-long affair with her late husband?"

She had a point, I had to admit. I hadn't really thought about how Muriel would feel. But I figured that Lilia's apology to her a few weeks back might have made this dinner possible.

The Enlightenment of Esther

Muriel isn't one to hold a grudge. Rosalie is much better at that.

"No, I hadn't, but I'll run it by Muriel tomorrow to see how she feels about it. Plus, I'll be taking Lilia to her stroke consultation on Wednesday, so maybe I'll have a chance to get to know her a little better."

Whoops. So much for not telling Rosalie about that little errand I had agreed to run.

"You're *what*?" she asked incredulously.

"Pete was supposed to take her, but he landed an interview at a financial firm for Wednesday and couldn't arrange for anyone else to take her."

"So, of course, he called you," Rosalie stammered.

"Hey, why don't you come with us?" I offered. "It'll be fun. Just you, me, and Lilia. We can go out for a nice lunch afterwards. I'll even spring for it. Any restaurant, your choice."

"You know, Esther. I wish I had jumped in after that shovel I dropped into Joe's grave. That would have been more fun than what you're proposing now."

"So, is that a yes?" I asked, already knowing the answer.

"No. And I warn you, Esther, if you invite them to Thanksgiving, you can count me out."

"Now really, Rosalie. You would break a fifty-year tradition over a couple of guests?"

"You wouldn't understand, Esther. You're only seventy-nine. But when you get to be eighty-five, that last thing you want is to be surrounded by a bunch of elderly, decrepit people on a holiday."

"Why, that's the silliest thing I ever heard. But if you really feel this strongly about it, then I won't invite any of them," I said.

Of course, I was going to invite all of them and just not tell

Rosalie that I did. I wanted to do a good deed here, and I wasn't going to let Rosalie's nonsense stop me. If, after she arrives for Thanksgiving, she decides to leave, then I can live with that. As they say in Spanish, *Que sera sera.* Whatever will be will be.

We arrived at the salon a few moments later, and since my appointment was before Rosalie's, I sat down in our stylist's chair and waited for him to perform his magic. Rosalie took a seat in the empty booth next to mine and started thumbing through a magazine.

"Well, hello, dear," Richard greeted me.

Richard is our stylist. He's in his forties, about six feet tall, blondish red hair, green eyes, and in very good shape.

"Good to see you," I said. "Just the usual for me, but Rosalie told me to tell you that she'd like to try some purple streaks in her hair. Kind of like what Cher did to her own hair not too long ago. Maybe spike it up a bit. Give her that punk rock look!"

Rosalie rolled her eyes.

"What do you say, Rosalie?" Richard asked. "Wanna give it a try?

"No," she said as she kept thumbing through her magazine.

"Richard," I continued, pivoting to the ubiquitous topic we Jewish mothers love to ask about, "now when are you going to settle down and find yourself a nice girl?"

"We've been over this, Esther. So unless you find me a girl that has a penis instead of a vagina, it'll never work out. Besides, I'm dating someone. He's absolutely dreamy."

"Well, umm, you never know. Maybe it's just a phase?" I asked.

"No, dear. I prefer dicks to chicks," he replied without missing a beat.

"So, you're dating someone?" I asked, as a peace offering.

"Well, do the two of you have any plans for Thanksgiving? I'd love to have you two over for the holiday."

I did this just to get a rise out of Rosalie. She's so predictable, and it's so easy to ruffle her feathers, and sure enough, she glared at me. But truth be told, I had no problem with having Richard and his, umm, date having a meal with us. Richard has been doing my hair for the last ten years, ever since my last stylist fell over dead from a heart attack right here on the salon floor. Very sad story. She had real talent.

"Why, Esther, dear, I'll see if he wants to come. I know I'd love to. You know my parents and I aren't exactly on speaking terms these days, and neither are his from what he's told me."

"Well, good. You just let me know. You're looking so thin these days. We need to get some meat on those bones," I said.

Rosalie glared at me again, or perhaps her glare had never stopped. Either way, I knew I was going to get an earful on the way home.

16

I woke up the next morning and started getting ready to head over to Sarah's. Another day of caretaking lay ahead of me, and I wasn't exactly looking forward to it. Sarah was a handful, even for the two of us to manage. But somehow, we muddled through it each and every day we were there. I just wish we had some additional help. If I had the power to, I'd smite Rosalie down where she stood, and Phyllis too. How both of them could have been so little help to me and Muriel was really starting to irritate me. And when Esther Kellerman gets irritated, you had better watch out.

Muriel called me as I was finishing getting dressed to tell me that Sarah seemed to be a bit more lucid today. She hadn't tried even once to fix Muriel's hair! Maybe this day will turn out all right after all.

I arrived at Sarah's a little after 10 a.m., and Muriel was absolutely right. Sarah was indeed more coherent than I had ever seen her. Well, I was glad for her having a good day so far. It'd certainly make our job easier. Muriel had fixed a late breakfast for both of them, so I went into the kitchen to clean up the dishes so that Muriel could rest a bit.

"I know you," Sarah said to me as she walked into the kitchen.

"Yes, dear," I responded. "We've spent quite a bit of time together over the last month or so. I'm Esther."

"Yes, Esther, I remembered that," she said unconvincingly.

"Well, I'm Sarah. Sarah Kellerman," she offered.

"No, dear. My last name is Kellerman," I corrected.

"Are we related?" she asked.

"No, I don't believe so. Your last name is Locker. You're Sarah Locker. And I don't believe I have any relatives with your last name."

"Oh, okay," she said, a bit deflated.

I could tell she was absolutely determined in her belief that her last name was Kellerman. I suppose I should be happy that she remembered any part of my name, even if she did try to claim it as her own.

"Here, why don't you come sit at the table, and we'll chat for a bit? Just let me finish up these dishes first," I offered.

This seemed to placate her for the moment, so I finished up the dishes while trying to keep an eye on her, since Muriel had conked out on the couch again. It still amazes me that Muriel thought she'd be up to task of taking care of an elderly patient. She's damned lucky to have me as a friend. That's all I can say.

"All right, Sarah," I said, taking a seat next to hers at the table. "Tell me about yourself."

You see, I wanted to really get to know Sarah's background, her life story. This was the first day since we've been looking after her that I thought she might be lucid enough to tell me about herself. On the few occasions that I've had the chance to talk to David and Dianne, I was never really able to get them to tell me much about her. I know she was a hairdresser, and I know her husband supposedly went to the store for eggs one day and never came back, but I really don't know much else about her.

Sarah just stared at me, clearly unsure of what to say or where to start, so I figured I'd do a little prodding.

"Have you always lived in the greater Columbus area? Were you born here?" I asked.

"No. Minnesota," Sarah responded.

"Ahh, Minnesota. Beautiful state," I added. "Was your family in Minneapolis or somewhere else in the state?"

"I, I don't know," she said.

"Well, that's okay," I reassured her. "People put too much stock in the names of cities."

"I, um, I think it was Minneapolis. Yes, yes, Minneapolis."

Well, at least we're getting somewhere. Sarah is from Minneapolis. I then asked her when she came to Ohio. Did she come with her family, or did she come alone? How old was she when she moved here? She could not remember the answers to any of these questions, but I thought maybe there was another way to reconstruct the timeline of her life.

"Do you remember if you were already living in Ohio when you got married? Did you meet your husband here?" I asked.

"Yes. I think I did. Yes, I know I did. I remember."

"Can you remember how you met?" I asked.

"I, I think we met somewhere."

"Do you remember where?"

She couldn't remember where they had met. But I started asking questions about their courtship, engagement, and wedding, and she remembered that her parents came from Minneapolis for the wedding. This means she must have moved here without them, but when I asked her to try and remember when and why she moved here, she couldn't. It doesn't matter, I suppose, but I do like a nice clean story with no loose ends, so I was a little disappointed.

"Tell me about your husband," I continued to prod. "What was he like?"

"He was kind. Handsome. Sometimes I couldn't hear him. He spoke softly."

Well, at least she seems to understand that he's no longer alive today, as she's talking about him in the past tense. That's progress, I suppose.

"What did he do for a living?" I asked.

"I, um," Sarah responded and then stopped talking.

"Dear, it's okay if you don't remember. I was married to my husband Joe for 49 years and 364 days, and sometimes even I forget that he was an accountant," I lied to her.

Sarah's eyes perked up a bit. I wasn't sure which part of what I had just said was registering with her, but I figured she was surprised that I had described the duration of our marriage to the day. So I explained to her what had happened to Joe on our fateful trip to Europe. She seemed to be comprehending at least some of what I was saying, and she actually laughed out loud when I was describing the actual incident of Joe being hit in the head and falling into the canal. Well, at least she still has some sort of appreciation for a humorous visual, never mind the fact that it ended in Joe's demise.

I noticed, though, that Sarah's attention was fading, and so I skipped over all of the details about getting Joe's body back to the States and planning the funeral and the shiva. I did tell her about Rosalie accidentally dropping the shovel in Joe's grave, and this brought out another grin on her face. I tell you, there's nothing better than seeing a smile on the face of someone you're looking after. I was glad that she was enjoying this moment.

"Rosalie," Sarah said.

"Yes, dear. Rosalie. Joe's older sister," I clarified.

"I want to see Rosalie," she added.

"Dear, I've been trying to get her to come over to meet you and sit with us for a while but she keeps refusing. I really have no idea why."

"I want to see Rosalie," she said again, rather insistently.

"Do you know a Rosalie?" I asked. "Perhaps I could find a number for a Rosalie you know. Maybe David and Dianne have an address book somewhere around here."

I told Sarah to just go ahead and stay where she was while I rummaged around the desk in the kitchen, looking for an address book. I came up empty-handed, however, and sat back down next to Sarah. The smile on her face was gone, and she was becoming quite agitated.

"Sarah, dear," I began. "Are you all right? Can I get you something to drink?"

She got up from her seat and started pacing around the kitchen. I yelled at Muriel to wake up and get herself in here to help me calm Sarah down, but my yelling did not produce its intended results. Muriel kept on dozing, so it was up to me to try to de-escalate the situation at hand. The problem was, I had no idea what to do, as I was pretty sure I wasn't going to be able to calm her down now by reading a book. She was too worked up.

Oh, if only Rosalie were here. She'd know what to do, having taken care of both her husband and her lover during their respective battles with the disease. I actually thought about calling her, but I didn't think that would go over well.

She'd probably berate me yet again for sticking my nose in where it didn't belong.

"Dear, what's the matter?" I asked Sarah as she continued to pace.

"My husband," she frantically responded.

"What about your husband, dear? Are you missing him?"

She nodded. I could tell she must have really loved her husband. I still don't know what happened to him, though. When did he pass away, and how? What did he do for a living? Was he a good husband? A good father to David? What kind of man was he? These were the questions that were running through my mind.

"I left him," Sarah said.

"What do you mean?" I asked, totally stunned.

I had no idea what she was talking about. Then again, I realized that I had assumed her husband passed away some years back. It never even occurred to me that their marriage had ended any other way than in his death. And now's she's telling me that she left him! Most women in our generation didn't leave their husbands. Divorce was much rarer then.

I knew someone who had divorced her husband because he was considered to be a little slow, mentally speaking. He didn't even drive! The marriage was her mother's idea because she was well into her twenties, still unmarried, and her youngest sister had just gotten engaged. You see, her mother figured that she would have a better chance later in life to find a good husband if she were a divorcee rather than an old maiden.

Oh, I also had a friend who divorced her husband because he was a serial gambler. He even tried to gamble away a "free night" with my friend in a bet at a poker game. When the winner came knocking the next day, she had her way with him since he was strikingly good-looking, and then she promptly called a divorce lawyer. I don't know what I would have done if Joe had bet a free night with me during a poker game. Well, okay, I probably wouldn't have slept with the winner, but you never know, I suppose. We all have our secrets!

"I left him," Sarah repeated.

"Yes, dear, I understood that part. But why? When?" I asked, becoming more confused.

"I, I, don't remember. What year is it?" she asked.

"Nineteen eighty-nine," I replied.

"No, it was after that," she responded, clearly having trouble understanding how linear time works.

"I'm sorry, dear, but it couldn't have been after 1989. It had to have been before. Probably long before. Your son made it sound like you had been living by yourself for some time," I explained.

"My son? You know it's a boy?" she asked, as she began to rub her stomach.

The only guess I had as to what was happening now was that Sarah seemed to be tying her leaving her husband with her pregnancy, at least in terms of when both events had occurred. I was starting to have a clearer picture of what might have happened, though I still wasn't sure of why. Sarah must have cheated on her husband, and when she found out she was pregnant with her lover's child, she must have left her husband.

Now I've heard of married women who have tried to pass off their illegitimate children as legitimate, but it hasn't always worked out so well in the end. Sooner or later, the truth usually comes out, whether it's from a blood test or from a particular trait or characteristic. My guess is that Sarah chose to run instead.

"But, Sarah, why did you leave your husband?" I asked, hoping for some sort of confirmation of my theory.

"I, I, he would have thrown me out," she answered.

"Where did you go?" I asked, very interested in anything she could tell me now.

"Here," she responded.

"Here to this house?" I asked, not really understanding how she could have come to this house back then.

"Here. Minneapolis."

17

I woke up the next morning with a splitting headache that was probably the result of what I can only describe as a hellacious ending to my day yesterday. I couldn't get Sarah to remember anything else about her past. She spent the entire afternoon convinced she was pregnant and was jubilant at the notion that she was going to give birth to a boy. She kept asking me who I was and what time did I expect her parents to return home from church.

Nothing I said could change her mind, and yes, I know you're supposed to just go along with whatever the demented person is saying. But I could only do that for so long before I just couldn't take it anymore. I called David and Dianne and asked him if he could come home and handle the situation. You see, I was hoping that Sarah would recognize him as her son and realize that she wasn't pregnant after all. If I could get him back here, maybe it'd be enough to snap her back into the present, or at least some version of the present in which she was no longer pregnant.

When David arrived home, I went over everything that had happened. Muriel had already gone home for the evening, so it was just me and David. Sarah was taking a nap right where Muriel had dozed off earlier in the day, on the couch in the living room.

I asked David if it was true what Sarah had said about learning she was pregnant and leaving her husband, his father. David didn't deny it, but he didn't elaborate either. I swear, it was like pulling teeth to get even the tiniest morsel of information out of him. I mean, who does he think he is? I'm doing him a big favor, not the other way around.

Anyway, that's enough about yesterday. Time to get the day started and prepare for my very important errand, taking Lilia Matthews to her stroke specialist consultation. I tell you, It feels like I have old ladies coming right out of my hair these days, but I have to say, it's a good feeling to feel useful again. Useful and exhausted.

As I sat down to drink my morning coffee, the phone rang, but I didn't even have to pick up the receiver to know who it was.

"Hello, Rosalie," I said.

"How did you know it was me?" she asked.

"Why, who else would be brazen enough to call this early in the morning? Only Rosalie the Riveter."

"Who?" she asked.

"Oh, that's just my little nickname that I call you inside my head."

"Kind of has a ring to it. Maybe I should have that put on my headstone," she laughed.

"I'm glad to hear you're in a better mood today. You were, umm, a bit cranky when we were at the salon the other day."

"Yes, I suppose I was," she responded. "Anyway, I was calling to see what you were up to today. I thought maybe we could have lunch and take in a movie."

I so wanted to avoid having Bitchy Rosalie resurface, but I suppose I had better be honest about what I was up to today.

"Rosalie, now don't get upset. I'm taking Lilia to her stroke specialist consultation today since Pete has an interview for a new job. But how about dinner and a movie instead? My treat!"

She hung up on me. I dialed her back, but she didn't pick up. I dialed her again, and she still didn't pick up. I dialed her a third time, and she finally answered, figuring I wasn't going to let up.

"*What?*" she yelled through what sounded like tears.

"Rosalie, sometimes I really don't understand you. It's clear you still have unresolved feelings over whatever happened to your sister, but the only thing that Lilia Kellerman and Lilia Matthews have in common is a shared first name. Why don't you come with us today? I really could use your help with her."

"I can't. I'm busy," she lied.

"Rosalie, you just asked me to lunch and a movie. I know your schedule is wide open today, so don't try to pull a fast one over on old Esther Kellerman. She's too smart to fall for it," I said, speaking of myself in the third person.

"Ha!" Rosalie replied. "I'm older than Esther Kellerman is, and I'm a whole lot wiser than she is, too. I'd never get myself mixed up in the quagmires she finds herself stuck in on an increasingly regular basis."

"Well, maybe Rosalie should live and let live, and just maybe she should try being a little more supportive of her sister-in-law's endeavors to try and bring a little kindness and humanity back into the world."

"Kindness and humanity are overrated," Rosalie responded.

"Well, anyway," I said. "I'll give you a call once I'm back

from my errand with Lilia. We can still do dinner and a movie if you'd like. I've been wanting to see that *Look Who's Talking* movie."

"I'll see if I can squeeze you in. I might find something better to do with my time, or at least a better movie to see," she teased.

"But, but, it's got talking babies in it! What could be cuter?" I asked.

"Nontalking babies," she deadpanned.

"Fine, pick a movie, and we'll go see it. Whatever you choose," I responded.

After hanging up the phone, I finished my now-cold coffee and headed to the bedroom to begin getting ready for the day ahead. I really didn't know what to expect. My interaction with Lilia had been very limited, and I did not yet have a good grasp on what her capabilities were. How much physical help would I need to provide her? If she fell, could I pick her up? How is she going to be able to communicate to the specialist what her abilities are? This was where I really wish Pete could have taken her because he'd be able to give the specialist a much more accurate description of Lilia's current physical and mental state.

I arrived at Pete and Lilia's about an hour and a half later, with more than a bit of trepidation. I really should have just rescheduled the appointment rather than try to take her myself, but since I was already here, I figured I'd better make the best of it. I rang the doorbell and waited for Pete to answer.

"Hello, Esther," Pete greeted me. "I can't thank you enough for agreeing to take my mother to the specialist."

"Well, diamonds are a girl's best friend," I hinted.

"Duly noted," Pete laughed. "When I start making the big bucks again, I'll buy you the biggest damned cubic zirconia money can buy."

"Pete, dear," I began. "I want the good stuff. The real diamonds, not diamond lookalikes."

"And you shall have it," he assured me. "I was just yanking your chain a bit."

"Well, don't," I said seriously.

"All right. Why don't you come on in while I finish getting Mother ready to go?"

So, after leading me inside, he asked me to take a seat in the family room while he went and finished up with Lilia. I took this opportunity to take my makeup compact out of my purse to do a little bit of touching up. It never hurts to look your best when you have an appointment with a medical professional. You never know when one might be in the market for a new love interest, and even though I was well past the age of caring about such matters, I do have three granddaughters to think of, and it'd be nice if at least one of them would marry a good Jewish doctor.

Actually, I wouldn't even mind if one of them married a gentile doctor. Just so long as he's a kind man and makes a good living. To me, that little abbreviation before his name was far more important than whether he was properly circumcised or not. Don't get me wrong. I wouldn't exactly call myself a fan of interfaith marriages, but I'm not one to look down upon those who do decide to enter into one. Love has a funny way of working out the way it was meant to.

Just as I was finished touching up my lipstick, Pete and Lilia came into the room. Pete was dressed in an impressive, double-breasted black suit, white dress shirt, and a yellow tie with little ducks on it. Lilia was dressed in powder-blue slacks with a white blouse and a gray cardigan sweater over it. Her silver hair had been tamed into a pageboy style and actually complimented the outfit. I was impressed that Pete had been able to make Lilia look so presentable.

"Hello," Lilia managed to eke out.

"Hello to you too, dear," I responded in kind. "That's a lovely sweater you're wearing today. It really complements your hair."

She brought her one good hand up to her hair and gave me a weak smile, clearly pleased by my compliment.

"Well, Esther," Pete began, "let me help you get Mother situated into your car. It'll take a little while to get her out there, so we better go ahead and start now."

I agreed and got up from where I was sitting. Pete motioned to me to grab Lilia's purse from the counter, which I did, and I then followed them both out to my car. Slowly. She can walk with her walker, thank goodness, but her gait is very short and halting. I really hoped the specialist would be able to give her some hope or at least some encouragement today.

Pete got Lilia situated into the passenger seat and buckled her up. He then asked me to open the trunk so he could put her walker inside, which I did. I was about to ask him if there was anything in particular I should say to the specialist on Lilia's behalf, but he preempted me by saying he had forgotten to bring out a sheet of paper on which he had written some "talking points," as he called them. He went back inside to fetch the paper.

"Well, Lilia," I began, "I hope you don't mind me calling you 'Lilia.' I'm so glad we're going to have the day to get to know each other. Your son seems like such a mensch. Well, except for the whole money extortion thing, but I've learned to overlook that. Do you know what the term 'mensch' means? It means a person with honor, integrity, and just a stand-up character."

She nodded as if she already knew what it meant. She took my hand and grasped it. Really a very warm gesture for someone she didn't even know. As she continued to hold my hand, I started getting the feeling that there was something she wanted to say to me, to communicate to me, but couldn't. I was going to have to find some way to figure out how to understand her, some way to read her thoughts. You know, you can tell a lot about what a person is trying to say just by reading their body language. I guess I was going to have to give it a try with Lilia.

Pete came back out a moment later with the piece of paper, and then we were off. The specialist was about twenty minutes away, so we had some time to try to get to know each other. I didn't really know how to accomplish this with her, but I thought that maybe I could start with some yes or no questions. This way, all she had to do was nod or shake her head in response.

So, I began with some simple questions. I asked her if she was originally from the area. She nodded. I asked her if she liked the crisp fall weather we were experiencing. She nodded. I asked her if she wanted me to turn up the heat. She shook her head. This was going brilliantly so far!

"Okay, Lilia," I said next. "I'm going to ask you an open-ended question, and I want you to answer as best as you can with your voice. Ready?"

She nodded.

"Why did you sleep with Muriel's husband? Is it because you were a wanton slut? Or were you just lonely and looking for some company?"

She turned her head towards me, eyes wide open in disbelief that I would ask her this. Well, of course I would ask her this! Muriel is a dear friend of mine, and Lilia had been party to a grievous emotional injury that Muriel had sustained. In truth, though, what I was really looking for was her reaction. You can tell a lot about a person by seeing how they react to being attacked for something they admittedly have done. Yes, she apologized to Muriel, but I wanted to see how she would react to me. I wanted to see if she'd toe that contrite line of sorrow, or whether she'd try to defend herself now that Muriel wasn't present.

"I, my husband," she said with great difficulty.

"Yes, dear, go on. What about your husband?"

"He died," she responded.

"And? What does his death have to do with Muriel's husband?"

"He, he saved me," she managed to eke out.

"From what? From money issues?" I asked, taking a stab in the dark, remembering what Pete had said about Lilia only having to work part time in order to be home with him as much as possible.

She nodded.

"Well, since Muriel seems to have forgiven you, I guess I will as well," I offered. "I don't know what it's like to be financially desolate. I suppose you were doing what you thought you had to in order to raise and support your son."

She nodded again. Now I wondered whether Pete's father was Muriel's late husband or Lilia's late husband. Oh, this was getting confusing.

18

We spent the rest of the car ride in silence and arrived on time for Lilia's appointment. I parked the car, got out, and then opened the trunk to retrieve Lilia's walker. She was able to unbuckle herself and open the door without assistance, but she needed a little bit of help getting out of the car and onto her walker. I shut the passenger door, locked the car, and then the two of us made our way into the doctor's office.

I sat Lilia down in a seat and then went up to the front desk to check her in. The woman behind the counter gave me a clipboard with some paperwork to fill out, but I told her the situation and said we'd fill out as much as we can—if the doctor wants a complete medical history for Lilia, he's going to be sorely disappointed, I'm afraid.

When I sat down next to Lilia, she took the clipboard from me with her good hand and started filling it out herself. I suppose Pete did say her cognition was pretty good, and I had to assume that her unaffected hand was also her dominant hand.

She was lucky in that regard. I couldn't imagine having a stroke and losing the use of my writing hand, along with most of my speech. That would seriously limit my ability to communicate and order people around. Oh, who am I kidding? Rosalie's the one who'd be out of luck there. She thinks she's the boss of everybody just because she's the oldest in the family.

I couldn't help but peer over to see how Lilia was getting along filling out the form, and I noticed that there was a spot on the form for her maiden name. I didn't know why the doctor needed to know what her maiden name was, but Lilia left it blank anyway. Now, how does someone not remember her own maiden name? I pointed to that particular question on the form and looked at Lilia with a quizzical stare.

"What is it, dear?" I asked. "Are you having trouble remembering your maiden name?"

She nodded.

"Just make something up then. They'll never know. Hell, just take my last name. We can pretend to be related."

I then spelled my last name for her, and she reluctantly wrote it down. For a brief moment, I wondered how Rosalie would feel about me letting Lilia Matthews pretend to have once been Lilia Kellerman, but as usual, what Rosalie doesn't know won't hurt her. Hopefully I'll remember not to say anything about it to her. I don't like keeping secrets from Rosalie, but it's her own damn fault for being so stubborn when it comes to judging what she thinks I should and should not do or get involved in. Serves her right!

As Lilia continued to fill out the form, she got stuck on the family medical history section. The form was asking for her parents' names and medical histories, but she seemed to be drawing another blank.

"Dear, do you not know your parents' medical histories?" I asked.

She nodded.

"Were you adopted?" I followed up.

She nodded, but she did it in a way that unnerved me a bit. It was almost like someone had just presented her with a brilliant idea that she was agreeing to, rather than nodding in truth. But why would she lie to me about this? I thought about pressing her on it, but I wasn't sure what good it would do at this point. For whatever reason she had, I could see that I was not going to get her to fill out the family medical history portion of the form. If she wanted to pretend to have been adopted, that was fine by me. No skin off my shoulder.

Once Lilia was done with the rest of the form, or should I say the portions she was willing to fill out, I took the clipboard and form back up to the receptionist's desk. Lilia and I then waited for a few moments longer before someone called her name. And when I looked up to see who it was, well, let's just say I should have seen this coming. Seems like my life is just a bunch of accidental acquaintances these days.

"Well, hello, Dianne," I said.

"Mrs. Kellerman, it's wonderful to see you! Have you been expanding your newfound caregiving career?" Dianne asked, pointing to Lilia.

"No, dear," I said, trying to figure out how to explain who Lilia was to her. "Lilia is, well, she's a relative. My sister-in-law."

Okay, so that was a lie, but I figured since I let her borrow my last name, I might as well take the ruse a step further. Both Dianne and Lilia just looked at me, but neither one said a word. I guess Dianne was questioning my sincerity. How dare she, I chuckled to myself.

Dianne escorted us back to an exam room and took Lilia's vitals, which all checked out okay.

"So, this is the doctor's office you work in? But I thought you usually work for a general practitioner. Haven't I called you there before? I have to admit, I'm just a little bit confused."

"No it's okay. I fill in here once in a while when the caseload is light at the GP's office. My first professional job was working as a neuro ICU nurse, so I have the necessary skills to work here as well."

"But, honey, why not just work here full-time then?" I asked, still feeling a bit dazed.

"The benefits aren't as good. The partners of the practice aren't as generous here," she said, though I wasn't sure I actually believed her. Something just didn't feel right.

"Oh, before I forget, Mrs. Kellerman, I found someone to sit with Sarah five days a week starting next Monday, so we won't be needing you and Muriel to come in at all after the end of this week. But we want you to know how appreciative we are of everything you two have done for us. I was going to call you tonight to let you know, but I hadn't counted on seeing you today!"

"Oh, that's wonderful news! I wasn't sure how much longer Muriel and I could keep it up. Well, more Muriel than me, since I'm a fair bit younger. I'll call Muriel and let her know this evening," I responded.

"Thank you," Dianne replied. "Looks like everything is in order here. I'll let the doctor know you're ready, and he'll be in in just a few moments."

Dianne then got up from her seat and left the room. I explained to Lilia exactly who Dianne, David, and Sarah Locker were. She looked at me, wanting to ask a question I think, but seemingly unable to find her words. Seeing her struggle so made me really wonder what it must feel like to be trapped in one's own body. Lilia clearly still has all her marbles, but her body just won't cooperate.

We waited for a bit, so I decided to start asking some questions of Lilia that I thought might be pertinent. I asked her if she thought she could improve on her current abilities. She nodded. I asked her if she felt that her son was taking good care of her. She nodded. I asked her if she had ever heard of any of the Lockers before. She nodded.

"Really?" I asked. "How do you know Sarah, David, and Dianne?"

She shook her head.

"Okay, maybe there's one of them you know?"

I then went through all three, and the only one she nodded to was Sarah. So, somehow, Lilia knew Sarah. At first, I thought, maybe they were childhood friends, but that didn't make sense to me for two reasons. First, Sarah is a bit older than Lilia. And second, Lilia was born and raised here, but Sarah was born and raised in Minneapolis. So how did they know each other?

I was about to ask some more probing questions along this line, but the doctor came in and interrupted my train of thought.

"Hello, ladies," he said. "I'm Dr. Shepard."

"Pleasure to meet you," I responded. "And this is Lilia Matthews, your patient. I'm just her ride."

"So, Mrs. Matthews," Dr. Shepard continued. "I've been taking a look at your medical history form, and I'd like to perform a comprehensive evaluation on you. We'll do some of it today, and we'll schedule some tests for later as well. But right now, I'd like to test your motor skills with a few simple exercises to give me a clearer picture of where your baseline is. Would that be all right?"

She nodded.

Dr. Shepard then proceeded through his battery of exercises with Lilia. He started by asking her to touch her nose with both her right and left index finger. She could only do it with the left. He then asked her to place the palms of her hand against his and told her to push with all her strength. She was able to keep his right hand from moving using her left hand, but she couldn't do the same on the other side. Next, he asked her to straighten each leg out completely. Again, she could do it with her left leg, but not her right—or at least she couldn't hold her right leg up to straighten it out. It's quite possible she could have straightened it if she were sitting on the floor.

"Well, Dr. Shepard," I began, "is there any hope for improvement?"

"To be honest, I don't know yet. I won't know for sure until we do an MRI," he responded. "Do you both know what an MRI is?"

I thought that I did, but I figured I'd ask Dr. Shepard to elaborate. You know, for Lilia's sake.

"We're going to do an MRI on your brain, Mrs. Matthews," he started to explain. "This is a very powerful scan that will help me to see exactly how much damage was done to your brain from the stroke you had. You'll be placed in a tube, where you have to lie very still for a period of time. This is necessary to ensure that the MRI is performed accurately. It's a fairly new tool in the medical field, really just within the last several years in terms of widespread usage."

I asked Lilia if she was interested in having the procedure done. She nodded.

"There's just one little hiccup," Dr. Shepard warned Lilia. "Because your stroke was twenty years ago and you have presumably had no additional strokes or any symptoms to indicate that you have had another one, we might have a problem getting Medicare to cover the cost."

"Money is not a concern," I reassured them both. "If Lilia needs an MRI, then she's going to get one. Let me, umm, illustrate my point a bit further. A few years ago, I accidentally grazed a neighborhood kid with my Cadillac. He was riding his bicycle where he shouldn't have, and my right-hand mirror skinned his left elbow. As a result, I will be paying for his entire college education. So believe me when I say that money is no object."

Both Lilia and Dr. Shepard looked at me with expressions of shock and awe on their faces.

"Mrs. Matthews," Dr. Shepard said, after he regained his composure, "you are a very lucky lady to have such a dear friend."

Lilia smiled in appreciation at me. I really hadn't considered Lilia a friend. Not even close. I mean, she slept with my dear friend's husband, for goodness sake! But I decided the moment called for me to play along, so I did.

"Listen," Dr. Shepard continued. "I think it's a good idea to get you into some speech and physical therapy even before we do the MRI. I won't know for sure how much improvement, if any, can be made until we do that MRI, but based on what I am seeing today, I do believe there's cause for hope. Now mind you, I'm not talking about a complete recovery to where you were before the stroke twenty years ago, but I think meaningful improvements can still be made. Especially with your speech. Speaking of which, you haven't said a word, so let's see what you can do now."

Lilia nodded.

"Please repeat the following sentence: I am very hungry."

She was able to get the whole sentence out, but not very smoothly.

"Please repeat the following sentence: I am tired."

Lilia had less trouble with this one.

"Please repeat the following sentence: I am thirsty."

Lilia had more difficulty with this one. Dr. Shepard explained that it has to do with the movements within the mouth and the tongue that are necessary to form letters and syllables. Some are easier than others, so it's less about the length of the sentence and more about the letters and words themselves. I guess I really hadn't thought of speech in such a manner before. But he was making a lot of sense.

"Speech therapy will give you back some of those letters and sounds that you're having trouble making. You may or may not be able to speak more quickly, but I am hopeful that you will be able to speak more clearly," Dr. Shepard explained.

Lilia, probably for the first time in a long while, seemed hopeful.

"All right, Dr. Shepard," I said. "Just tell us where to go for this speech therapy, and we'll get her started on it. Oh, and what about the MRI? How do we get that scheduled?"

"So, the MRI will have to be done at the hospital, but I'll get you connected with the imaging department to set that up. Regarding the speech therapy, we'll put in a referral for you. We have working relationships with several speech therapists in the area, all of whom are excellent in what they do."

"Is there anything else we should be doing?" I asked.

"We'll know more once we see the MRI," Dr. Shepard ended.

19

I dropped Lilia off after the appointment was done, and thankfully, Pete was already back from his interview so I didn't have to wait around for him to return.

"So, how'd the interview go?" I asked Pete as I helped Lilia get back into the house.

"I have a really good feeling about it, Esther," he responded. "They said they'd let me know sometime next week, but I could tell by the smiles on their faces that I was their new top candidate."

"That's wonderful news, Pete!" I said. "I'm so happy for you, and so is my checkbook! Now I just have to figure out how to make Muriel solvent again financially, and we'll be in business."

"About that, Esther," Pete added. "Assuming I do get this job, I'd like to start helping her out. We've taken so much from her, and it's time to give back a little if we can."

Lilia nodded in agreement.

"I think that would be a lovely idea," I said. "Now whether Muriel would take money from you, I don't know. But I can be

The Enlightenment of Esther

pretty persuasive when I want to be, and I'll find a way to convince her."

"So, did the appointment with the specialist go well?" Pete asked.

Lilia tried to answer him, but she wasn't really able to speak clearly enough to give him the details, so I told him about her needing speech therapy for starters and then an MRI to see how much improvement she might be able to make. When he started to ask about the cost of the MRI, I told him not to worry about it and that I would take care of it. He was very thankful and very relieved.

"Oh, Pete," I then added. "Before I forget, I would love it if you and your mother would join me and my family for Thanksgiving this year."

They looked at each other with some trepidation. Maybe they were just used to spending the holidays by themselves, but I was a little bit unsettled by their reaction to my gracious invitation.

"You'll have a chance to meet my daughter and son-in-law and their daughters. My sister-in-law Rosalie should be there, too. Muriel will probably join us, too, since her daughters are going elsewhere for the holiday, and I've even invited Sarah and her son, David, and daughter-in-law, Dianne. Did I mention Sarah to you the other day? The woman Muriel and I have been looking after? Oh, and I invited my hairdresser, Richard, too. It'll be an eclectic gathering, but I'm sure you'll enjoy yourselves."

Neither Pete nor Lilia said a word. I was starting to wonder if I was speaking gibberish to them and didn't know it.

"Umm, we really do appreciate the invitation, Esther. We'll discuss it and let you know soon. We're not used to spending holidays with anyone else but ourselves, but it might be a nice change for us," Pete said.

Lilia gave him a stern look—a look that actually reminded me so much of the look Rosalie gives me every time I get involved in something I shouldn't.

"Just let me know within the next week or two so that I can make sure I plan for enough food for everyone," I said.

"Speaking of food," Pete said, "why don't you stay and have some lunch with us? I've got deli meats, good rye bread, cheeses, chips, and some homemade half-sour pickles."

"You make your own pickles?" I asked, taken by surprise.

"I sure do!"

"Well, I'm a sucker for a good half-sour pickle, so I'll stay. Thank you."

Lilia reached out and grabbed my hand. Ugh, I still couldn't believe I was befriending the woman who Muriel's late husband had an affair with. But she seemed so touched that I was willing to help her out, and I figured she didn't have many friends of her own on account of her health. So I took a seat next to her at the table while Pete went about fixing our lunch.

"Esther," Lilia said, with great effort. "Your... husband."

I asked her if she wanted to know about my husband, and she nodded. So I told her all about Joe. I told her about his career and our wonderful 49-year- and 364-day-long marriage, and of course I told her about how he passed away. I tried to spin it in a humorous way, but it seemed that I had failed because she started tearing up. I wonder if Mr. Matthews had died in a similar accident, but I doubted her husband had fallen off of a gondola. That would have been too much of a coincidence.

"Rosalie?" Lilia asked after I had finished telling her about Joe.

The Enlightenment of Esther

I told her all about Rosalie, her husband, her lover, and how both of them had been afflicted with dementia. I probably shouldn't have, but I told her about Rosalie's disapproval of my helping her out. This brought more tears to Lilia's eyes. I guess anyone would be hurt finding out someone didn't want you to get the help that you so desperately needed. I tried to reassure her that Rosalie was just set in her ways, but that didn't stop the tears from flowing.

I got up and asked Pete for a napkin or a tissue for Lilia. But when I got near enough to him, I could see a few tears welling up in his eyes as well. But why? I wondered. Why are they both acting like all the joy in the world has been lost? He pointed to a wire basket on the countertop that held a stack of napkins, so I grabbed one and brought it back to Lilia.

"Esther," Pete began, trying to wipe away the tears. "I've got corned beef, pastrami, and turkey. What would you like? Or would you like all three?"

"Oh, corned beef sounds good. With a little mustard and mayo if possible," I responded.

"Coming right up," he said as he wiped away the last of his tears.

Lilia was looking at me very intensely again, so I asked her if there was something she wanted to say. She nodded and pointed to a pad and pen on the other side of the table. It took me a few seconds to realize that she wanted to write down what she wanted to say, but I finally got the picture and handed her the pad and pen.

After she finished, she handed me the pad, and I read it aloud.

"Did Joe have a wife before you?" the pad asked.

I thought that was an odd question to ask, but I told Lilia

that no, Joe didn't have a wife before me. She gestured to me to hand the pad back to her, and she started writing again.

"Is Rosalie your late brother's wife?" the pad asked next.

My, she was really delving into my family tree now. I told her that Rosalie was Joe's sister and that I had never had a brother. Seems like she would have realized this when I was telling her about Rosalie's husband earlier. I would have mentioned that he had been my brother at that time. She then motioned for the pad again.

"Did Joe and Rosalie have any other siblings?" the pad wanted to know.

I told her that, yes, they had five sisters, four of whom are still living. I handed the pad back to her before she could motion for it again.

"What happened to the fifth sister?" the pad wondered.

I told Lilia that I didn't know much, other than that the family had mourned her death years ago, before I even met Joe. No one would ever talk about her. I debated whether to tell Lilia that she shared a name with the deceased sister, but I figured I'd better keep that to myself. Lilia was tearing up again. Maybe she had a sister once upon a time who also died young.

I passed the pad back to her just as Pete was bringing our lunches to the table. As she started writing again, Pete asked me what I would like to drink. I told him a good stiff scotch would do, but he said he'd rather not serve me any alcohol since I'd be driving home soon after lunch was over. I suppose he was right, but I was a little disappointed. I said a Coke would suffice then, and he went back into the kitchen to fetch a can for me.

When he returned with my Coke, Lilia handed the pad to him.

"We're taking Esther up on her offer for Thanksgiving," the pad said.

The Enlightenment of Esther

Pete looked surprised and asked her if she was sure. She nodded determinedly.

"Well, it looks like we'll be joining you and your eclectic gathering for Thanksgiving," Pete said to me. "When Mother has made her mind up to do something, there's no stopping her!"

I reached over to Lilia and grabbed her hand in an attempt to show her I was really looking forward to having both of them there. And I meant it. This poor woman had been trapped in her own body for twenty years, and I was glad to have had a part in giving her some real hope for the first time in a long while.

"Try your pickle," Pete nudged me.

I took the pickle in one hand, and it almost slipped through my fingers. Slippery little thing. Well, not so little, I suppose. Actually, the pickle had a very satisfying depth, or width, or diameter, or whatever the appropriate term is. I picked it up again and held it between my thumb and two fingers and took a big bite. Thank goodness it was just a pickle! Oh, what a pickle of a situation I would have found myself in if it were anything but a pickle!

"It's a good pickle, isn't it?" Pete asked.

It was absolutely delicious, and to communicate this to him, I started moaning. He started laughing out loud. I tell you, I was really having a nice time with Pete and Lilia. I guess you're never really too old to make new friends. If, God forbid, I should ever have to be in a nursing home, I think I'll be okay.

Pete helped Lilia with her meal while I ate mine. The corned beef sandwich was tasty, and the chips were my favorite flavor. Sour Cream and Onion. I was so genuinely touched by watching Pete take such great care of his mother, making sure she didn't take bites that were too big for her to swallow. I started to wonder why Pete was single. Seems like he would have made a woman an excellent husband, from what I could tell.

Now I'm sure you're wondering by now if I have the gumption to ask him why he never settled down with a wife of his own. Well, I do, and I did. He said he just hadn't met the right person and didn't want to settle for someone less than what he wanted or thought he deserved. In my day, you only settled for not getting married if you couldn't find a living body to drag down the aisle to the altar. But times have changed, and maybe for the better.

I took my leave of them shortly after we finished lunch and told them to just let me know about the speech therapy appointments for Lilia and when she would need someone to take her. Since I was going to be done with looking after Sarah in a couple of days, I'd be available to continue helping out with Lilia.

I got in my car, put the key in the ignition, and . . . nothing. Damn, the car wouldn't start. I was just getting a repetitive clicking sound. I knew it couldn't be the battery since the car was so new, but I didn't know what else it could be. So I got out of the car, walked back up to Pete and Lilia's front door, and knocked.

When Pete opened the door, I said, "You sold me a lemon! The damn thing won't start!"

He took the keys from me, got into the car, and tried to start it himself, but to no avail. He walked back up to me and asked me if I had any jumper cables, which I didn't. I then asked him if he had any, though I figured if he had had some, he wouldn't have asked me if I did. As expected, he didn't.

"The way I see it," he began, "we've got two options. We can call the dealership and have the car towed there now. You could ride over with the tow truck driver and have someone pick you up from there."

"What's option two?" I asked.

"You leave the car here. I take care of your car tomorrow, and Mother and I drive you home now. You'd be without a car for the evening, though, versus getting a loaner from the dealership."

"Let's go with option two," I said. "I have plans with Rosalie tonight, and she can drive us instead. No problem. I'll leave the car in your capable hands. But let me give you Sarah's number so you can call me over there tomorrow when the car is fixed. Muriel and I will be sitting with her for most of the day."

"Okay. Come back into the house so I can write it down and get Mother ready for the ride over to your place."

20

We left Pete and Lilia's and headed towards my home in Pete's Acura Legend. While it wasn't as nice as my nonstarting Saab is, or as nice as my mailbox-killing Cadillac was, I was comfortable enough in the backseat. Lilia offered the front seat to me, but it seemed silly for her to have to change seats once they dropped me off, so I plopped myself down in the rear before either of them could object.

We drove on, and as we did, Pete was gaining more and more confidence that he had landed that job he interviewed for. He started regaling us with ever more elaborate answers he gave to the questions the interviewers posed to him. I couldn't see Lilia's face from where I was sitting, but her left hand kept patting Pete's right knee in approval. Most of what he said didn't make a whole lot of sense to me, but I kept up my end of the conversation with a bunch of "great point," "perfect response," and "they'd be fools not to hire you" responses. I just hoped in the back of my mind that his enthusiasm was really warranted.

As we began to approach my house, I noticed a white car

sitting out in front. As we got a little closer, I recognized the car as Rosalie's new mini Buick. And as we drew closer still, I saw a figure sitting on my front steps. Well, it didn't take a brain surgeon to put two and two together. I told Pete to go ahead and just pull behind her car and let me out at the curb.

Lilia was trying to ask something, but I had a hard time understanding her. It would have helped if I could have read her lips, but since I was still in the backseat, that wasn't possible. Pete kindly interpreted for me and said that his mother wanted to know who the woman sitting on my front steps was. Now, mind you, my front steps are a good thirty to forty feet away from the curb, so I wasn't sure what difference it would make to Lilia as to who the woman was, but I answered.

"That's Rosalie, the sister-in-law I've been telling you about."

Lilia turned her head to peer more intently out the window, and I tell you, it was like she was stuck, almost frozen in time. I looked more closely myself, but apart from Rosalie holding what looked like a photo album in her lap, I didn't notice anything unusual. But then I did notice something. I couldn't make out Rosalie's expression very well from this distance, but it seemed that she, too, was looking very intensely in our direction.

I thanked Pete and Lilia for the ride home and got out of the car, but before I closed the door, I turned and motioned to Rosalie to come over and meet them. She wouldn't budge, so I said my good-byes to Pete and Lilia and sent them on their way.

"I figured you'd be back sooner or later, so I decided to enjoy the nice weather we're having today," Rosalie explained.

"I can see that," I responded.

"You remember I mentioned showing you some pictures of my sister? Well, I thought now would be a good time, and then we can do dinner later. Not sure I'm up for a movie afterwards though."

"Come, let's go inside and have a nice chat over looking through these photos," I offered.

"Wait," Rosalie stopped me. "Where's your car? And who were those other people in the car you pulled up in?"

"My car wouldn't start, Rosalie, and I think you already know the answer to your second question," I said, grabbing her arm and helping her up from the steps.

"I see," she responded.

"I took Lilia home after her appointment was over, and I ended up eating lunch with her and Pete. When we were done, I left to drive home, but my car wouldn't start. Pete said he'd have the dealership come pick it up tomorrow from his house so they can figure out what's wrong with it."

I led the way into the living room and made sure Rosalie was comfortable. I asked her if she wanted something to drink as I was heading into the kitchen. She said she wouldn't mind a glass of wine, so I opened a bottle for the both of us. I suppose the polite thing would have been to ask her if she wanted red or white, but I thought, to hell with it. I wanted white, so that's what we were going to be drinking.

Rosalie came into the kitchen and started rummaging through my fridge for some snacks to go with the wine. I suggested that she take some red grapes out and wash them, while I sliced up some cheese and put out some crackers. I really wasn't hungry, but I'll never say no to cheese. We decided that maybe we should just move our little stroll down memory lane to the kitchen table, so I went back into the living room to grab the photo album.

I set the album on the table and went back to finishing up the cheese and crackers. Once everything was ready, we brought the wine, grapes, cheese, and crackers to the table. Rosalie took a healthy gulp of wine, and then another, and then another.

"Slow down, dear," I said, starting to get a bit alarmed. "Pace yourself. Here, eat some crackers before you make yourself sick."

"You're right," she said ashamedly. "It's just this whole other Lilia business you've gotten yourself mixed up in. It's brought back so many memories."

"Why won't anyone in this family ever talk about what happened to her? Not you. Not Joe. Not any of your other sisters. I've asked you before, but this time I'm not taking your silence as an answer. Whatever happened, unburden yourself now."

Rosalie opened the album, ignoring my plea, and started showing me pictures of her sister as a child. Now keep in mind, while cameras had become more widely available by the early 1920s, people weren't accustomed to taking gobs and gobs of pictures like they do today, so I wasn't sure just how many pictures of her sister were actually in this album.

"Here," Rosalie said, pointing to a picture of a beautiful little girl in a checkered jumper. "She must have been about seven or eight years old when this picture was taken. Even as a child, she could turn heads. If she had been born a decade later, no one would have ever known who Shirley Temple was."

"Such a precious picture," I offered, as Rosalie flipped to the next page.

"Oh, and here's a picture of Joe and Lilia together. I think this was taken on the day Joe graduated from high school so she must have been about ten years old. Lilia idolized him. She was so proud of him, and so was I. You know I was never able to finish school, but Joe did. I made sure of that. Come hell or high water, I was determined to make sure that all of my siblings graduated."

I looked over at Rosalie, and she was tearing up again. Rosalie asked for a tissue, so I went to fetch some for her. I needed to visit the bathroom anyway, but a funny thing happened on the way. You know how sometimes an idea will just hit you upside the head? Well, I started wondering about Lilia Kellerman and whether she was really dead after all. Not once in the 49 years and 364 days that I was married to Joe did we ever visit her grave. I suppose she could have been cremated, but that really does go against Jewish tradition, and the Kellermans were pretty observant of Jewish tradition even if they weren't overly religious themselves.

Rosalie had the album turned to another page when I came back, tissues in hand. She pointed to what looked like a family wedding photograph. I recognized the picture. This was taken at their mother's second wedding. She finally landed another man, but by then, the children were mostly grown up. I suppose that without a bunch of children to support, she became a worthier prospect for the men of her time.

I started looking at the faces of the family members in the picture, and I recognized nearly all of them. Their mother and newly minted stepfather were in the center, surrounded by the young adult versions of Rosalie, Joe, and their siblings. Rosalie's husband was next to her, and two of the other sisters were also married by this time, so their husbands were standing next to them as well.

The one person I didn't recognize was a woman standing next to Joe at the right end of the picture. She looked familiar, though, but I couldn't quite place her. There was something in her eyes that registered with me, but I didn't know where I had seen them before. I know I've seen this photograph before, but I honestly don't remember there being a woman whom I did not recognize standing next to him.

"Rosalie," I began as I pointed to the mysterious person in the picture, "who is this woman?"

Rosalie made a big production out of looking more closely at the picture, as if she didn't already know who all of the faces belonged to.

"Goodness, I don't believe I know," she responded. "Must have been an old girlfriend of Joe's."

"Rosalie, dear," I started to say. "Your mind is like a steel trap. I have a hard time believing you don't know who this woman was."

She took another look at the picture, and then even more unconvincingly said, "Nope."

"I guess that steel trap is getting a bit rusty and no longer closes all the way," I teased. Though to tell you the truth, I was starting to get a bit peeved.

"Let's move on," she gestured.

"Hold on. Wait a minute," I said, as I kept Rosalie from turning the page. "There's something about this woman. Something familiar. I can't place her, but I feel like I know her from somewhere."

"I highly doubt that," Rosalie replied.

"Who is she, Rosalie?" I pressed.

"How should I know?" she desperately responded. "This picture was taken nearly sixty years ago. How can you expect me to remember every single person in a sixty-year-old photograph?"

"There's something you're not telling me, Rosalie," I asserted, totally unconvinced by Rosalie's lies. "That photograph was taken only a few years before I met Joe. You must know who this woman was."

"I really don't," Rosalie flatly said.

"Here," I said, refilling her glass of wine and nudging it towards her. "Have another glass. It'll relax you."

Okay, so apparently I was not above getting Rosalie drunk in an attempt to pump her for information. Does that make me a bad person? A bad friend or a bad sister-in-law? Well, next time I see our sober friend from the book club who goes to Alcoholics Anonymous religiously, I'll ask her. Until then, I was absolving myself of all moral and ethical dilemmas involved with my present pursuit of knowledge.

Unfortunately, I must have gotten lost in my own thoughts because I hadn't noticed that Rosalie had sneakily flipped the album to the next page.

"Here," she said, pointing to a photograph on the bottom of the right-hand page. "This is the last picture that I have of Lilia. Probably the last picture that was taken of her, at least that I know of. She had just started dating the gentleman standing next to her, and believe me, he was even more handsome in person that he looked in this photo."

"What was his name?" I asked.

"Goodness, I don't really remember. Oh, she was crazy about him."

"Rosalie, drink up!" I said as I nudged the wineglass closer to her again.

"You think I don't know what you're trying to do, Esther?" she asked rhetorically. "I've had enough wine, thank you."

"Oh, all right. I give up. So what happened with Lilia and this gentleman? Was he the one you were referring to that night at the club? The one gentlemen suitor whom she was really interested in?" I asked.

"Yes, this is the one. They dated for six months, and then he proposed to her. But our mother and stepfather didn't approve of him. She broke off the engagement because it was tearing our family apart, but then we lost her shortly after that."

"Rosalie, please tell me this isn't going to be a 'she died of a broken heart' story. I know you too well, and you're too cynical for that," I said.

"No, she didn't die of a broken heart, but I do believe she lost whatever it was within her that made her such a shining light when she broke off the engagement."

"How did she die?" I asked, figuring Rosalie probably wasn't going to answer.

"It was very sudden, and that's all I intend to say," she responded.

"Listen," I began, changing the subject a bit. "Instead of going out for dinner, let's just order a pizza. I think we've both had enough to drink that we shouldn't be driving, so you should feel free to drink some more now. Think of wine as good brain juice. Maybe you'll start remembering some of these names and faces you say you've forgotten!"

21

I woke up the next morning and started getting ready to go over to Sarah's for my penultimate day as one of her caregivers. As I was sitting down to have my morning coffee, the phone rang.

"Hello?" I asked.

"Esther, it's Muriel. I'm feeling a bit under the weather today. I hate to ask you to have to do this, but would you mind flying solo today with Sarah?"

Now this is one of those moments in life when you consider what you really want to say, and then you disregard it entirely in order to say what is expected of you.

"Mind? Why would I mind? I mean, it's not like I had yesterday to rest up like you did. But, do I mind? No, not at all, Muriel," I said.

Okay, so perhaps I laid on a little guilt there, but I did say that I didn't mind. I deserve brownie points for that. Or better yet, a big chocolate brownie with vanilla ice cream, whipped cream, and a maraschino cherry on top!

"Thank you, dear," Muriel responded. "I'll be back tomorrow. I called David and told him he might have to stick around until you get there. He wasn't too happy about it, but he said he understood."

I hung up the phone and hastened my morning routine. I was over at Sarah's a half hour later to find a very relieved David. He practically already had one foot out the door when I arrived and didn't even say hello to me as I passed him on the way in. Oh, the nerve!

"Well, good-bye to you too then!" I shouted as he raced into the garage to his car. I just couldn't help myself!

I set my purse down on the kitchen table and went into the living room to see how Sarah was doing today.

"Hello, Sarah," I greeted her.

"Hello, umm—" she responded, having trouble remembering my name. I thought we were past this, but apparently not.

"I'm Esther. Do you remember me? I've been coming over for a while now and visiting with you while your son and daughter-in-law are at work during the day."

"I know who you are," she snapped at me.

"Well, that's good! You're having a good day! I'm so happy for you! Maybe we can get to know each other a little better today."

"I don't want you here!" Sarah screamed.

"Excuse me?" I asked, both hurt and offended.

"Why are you doing this to me?" she continued.

"Do what?" I was totally confused now.

"You're trying to take my husband away from me!" she yelled. "I won't let you!"

So, it would seem Sarah didn't actually know who I was. She was confusing me with some woman who must have been after her late husband sometime in the past. Damn. How was I going to get myself out of this one? I've been around Sarah long enough by now to know that when she gets this upset, there's really no way to talk her down. The only thing I could think of to do was to tell her flat out that I had never met her husband.

"Liar," she said in response to this.

I tried changing the subject. This didn't work.

"Get out of my house!" she fumed.

I had had enough. I picked up the phone and called Dianne. I figured she was already at work, whereas David would still be on his way. Once I got her on the phone, I explained the situation, and she said she would come home as soon as she could. I told her that I would wait here for thirty more minutes, but that I was leaving after that whether or not she had arrived. She got the hint and said she was on her way.

Meanwhile. I still had Sarah to deal with on my own for the next thirty minutes. She was shooting daggers at me with her eyes, and she was actually snarling. I thought about trying to check her pulse, as I was sure it was racing, but I was afraid she might try to bite me if I got too close. A friend of mine was in the hospital once, and she would become so disoriented at night that, on one occasion, she actually bit her nurse!

The only thing I could think of to do was just sit at the kitchen table and start reading, pretending to ignore Sarah in the hope that her mind would wander onto some other topic. There was a *People* magazine sitting on the table, so I picked it up and started flipping through the issue. The cover story was showcasing the heroes from the earthquake that hit San Francisco last month. These people helped rescue those trapped in their homes and in their cars due to falling buildings and bridges. I tell you, that picture of the top level of the Bay Bridge partially collapsing onto the bottom level was heartbreaking to see.

The Enlightenment of Esther

I took a glance over at Sarah, and she was still shooting those daggers at me, so I continued reading, but this time I read aloud. I was hoping to get her interested in the story about these heroes and that she would forget about her anger towards me for allegedly trying to steal her husband away from her. The woman is mad, I tell you. She told me herself that she left her husband, though I suppose she never did get around to telling me why. Maybe he really was having an affair, and Sarah chose to leave him over it. In any case, my plan of distraction didn't work.

"Just wait until Rosalie finds out about you," Sarah said to me. "She'll fix you."

"And just exactly who is Rosalie to you?" I asked, getting very impatient and losing my control.

"She's my, my . . ."

"Dear, it would really help me out if you could remember who your Rosalie is and how you know her," I said, trying to dial back my temper a bit.

"I, I don't know." Sarah responded.

"Well, when you figure it out, you just let me know. In the meantime, I'm going to return to reading my article."

No more Mrs. Nice Esther. I'm locked and loaded for bear!

"Well, I still don't like you going after my husband," Sarah responded, and then turned her head away from me.

I decided to continue reading the article out loud, hoping that just maybe Sarah would start to take an interest in it. She got up and turned on the television. But she didn't just turn it on. She turned the volume up as loud as it would go, presumably to drown out my reading the article aloud. Now I know I should have let it go, but I tell you, I was done. So I stood up, took the magazine with me, went over to where she was sitting, and started screaming the article into her ear.

At first, she pretended that she couldn't hear me. Then she pretended that it wasn't bothering her. And finally, she turned to me and slapped me across the face. I suppose I had that coming, but you know what I did? I slapped her back! She just stared at me wide-eyed, and it was in that moment that I realized where I had seen those eyes from that woman standing next to Joe in his mother's wedding photograph. Those same eyes were staring at me now.

But how could this be? It can't be. This has to be a coincidence. There's no way that the woman in the photograph is the same woman sitting before me now. Not possible.

I got up from the couch and started pacing the room.

"Is everything all right, dear?" Sarah asked me, forgetting that, a moment ago, she was spitting nails in my direction.

Talk about a role reversal. Now she was trying to comfort me! I couldn't stop pacing, and of course, Sarah's eyes were tracking my every move.

"Here," Sarah said, patting the seat next to her. "Come sit by me and I'll tell you a story."

Oh, for heaven's sake. Now she thinks I'm a child. Maybe her child. Who knows? I started to move back towards the sofa where she was sitting. But in a stroke of luck, the phone rang. Sarah stood up to answer it, but I waved her away and was thankfully much closer to the phone than she was.

"Locker residence," I said, answering the phone.

"Esther, it's Pete. I'm calling about your car."

"So, what's wrong with the lemon of a car you sold me?"

"It turns out there's a loose connection with the alternator, so it wasn't charging up the battery like it's supposed to while you were driving. It'll be fixed in a half hour or so and then I can drive the car back to you. Someone else will follow me and take me back to the dealership afterwards," Pete said.

"No need for that. Sarah and I have had a bit of an altercation, so her daughter-in-law is coming home and should arrive soon. Just drive the car to my house, and I'll drive you back to the dealership myself."

"Are you sure you don't mind?" he asked.

"Not at all," I insisted. "I'll see you in a bit then."

I hung up the phone and turned around to realize that Sarah had snuck up on me and was right in my face. There are those eyes again. Those eyes from the photograph. Oh, what was I going to do? Sarah isn't coherent enough to tell me exactly who she is, how she knows Rosalie, or even how she knew Joe. But I am certain that somewhere in that addled brain of hers lies the truth to all of these puzzling questions that keep running through my mind.

"Sarah," I began. "Let's go sit down on the sofa and have a little chat. I have some questions that I am hoping you can answer for me."

"Oh, okay," she responded.

As we sat back down, I started to ask her again if she could remember how she knows Rosalie. Unfortunately, she was lost again in her own mind, and there was no coaxing her back to me. I heard the garage door open and realized that Dianne had made it home, so I stood up to greet her at the kitchen door. But then a thought occurred to me, an idea of sorts, so I decided to sit back down. I couldn't guarantee success, but if executed properly, this plan just might work.

Diane walked into the house, set her purse on the countertop, and made a beeline for us. She started apologizing profusely for everything that had happened and that they would still pay Muriel for the full day. Well, Muriel wasn't here. I was. But I didn't say anything. I was too busy going through the steps of my little plan to get distracted by matters of money.

"Dianne," I said, "Sarah seems to have calmed down a bit. So why don't you go change out of your work clothes and take a few minutes to yourself. I'll still be here. Go on now! Go on!"

"Are you sure, Mrs. Kellerman?" she asked.

"Yes, perfectly sure."

"Well, all right then. I'll be back out in just a little bit," she said as she walked towards the other end of the house.

I sprang into action as soon as Dianne was out of sight. I leapt off of the sofa with the grace of a cheetah and swiftly walked over to the counter where Dianne's purse lay. Remember my previous attempt to find an address book awhile back? Well, I struck gold this time when I reached my hand inside of the purse. One way or the other, I was determined to find out whether Sarah's Rosalie is indeed my Rosalie as well.

After opening the address book, I flipped to the S section, as her married name is Sherman. No luck. No Rosalie Sherman was listed. I then had another thought, though, and I flipped to the K section. There was no Rosalie Kellerman listed. Damn. But I wasn't done yet! I turned to the R section and found a Rosalie with no last name listed. My jaw dropped when I read the phone number listed next to the name. I recognized that number. I've dialed that exact same number a million times over the years.

I heard footsteps coming from the bedroom area, so I quickly stashed the address book back into Dianne's purse, but I didn't have time to make it back to the sofa before she reentered the room. So, what was I to do but start fetching a glass of water for Sarah, pretending that she had asked for one.

When I brought the water to Sarah, she refused to take it. By this point, Dianne was already in the room, so I tried to convince Sarah that she had just asked for some water. Yes, I know it was a cruel thing to do, but I was desperate. Sarah still refused to take the glass from my hand, though. I tried as gently as I could to open her right hand and place the glass of water inside of it, but she didn't take too kindly to that. She finally did grasp the glass. And then she threw the water into my face. I supposed I deserved it.

Dianne was mortified, but I told her not to fuss over it. I walked into the kitchen to grab a towel to dry off my face, and then I marched myself out of their house and back towards my own.

22

I had half a mind to walk over to Rosalie's house and demand that she tell me exactly who Sarah is. But I had to get back home and wait for Pete to arrive with my car, so my tirade was going to have to wait. By the time I reached my front steps, I was so enraged that I tripped and nearly fell flat on my face.

Now I understood why Rosalie had been so adamant about not helping us out with Sarah's care. She was afraid Sarah would recognize her, and whatever secret both of them are holding on to would come out into the open. But whatever this secret is must have something to do with Joe.

After closing the door behind me, I headed into the kitchen to pour myself a stiff scotch. But then I remembered that I had offered to drive Pete back to the dealership, so the scotch would have to wait. I settled for a can of Coke and some cookies. Yes, I probably should eat something a bit more substantial, but it's been my experience that only chocolate and sugar will do when upset.

While I was waiting for Pete to arrive, I decided to call

The Enlightenment of Esther

Phyllis up and fill her in on this connection between Sarah, Joe, and Rosalie that I had uncovered. She picked up the phone after the second ring, and I started to explain. But I must have either been speaking too quickly or incoherently, or both, since Phyllis didn't seem to be processing what I was saying.

"Mom," she interrupted, "why don't you call me a little later when you've had a chance to calm down a bit? You're not making any sense."

"I'm telling you, dear, that your father and your aunt both knew Sarah many years ago. I don't know how exactly, but they did. She was clearly in that family photo from your grandmother's wedding to her second husband. I'd recognize those eyes anywhere now. She's standing right next to your father."

"But, Mom, we both have seen that family picture before. Dad is all the way on the right-hand side of it, and there's no other woman standing next to him."

"I'll call you back, dear," I said as I hung up the phone.

Since Pete still hadn't arrived, I thought I might still have enough time to break open the albums that I have and see if I can find my copy of that picture. Well, it was Joe's copy really. But it's mine now! But I realized I still had some cookies to eat, so I figured the albums would have to wait until I got back from dropping Pete off at the dealership. It was gnawing at me though. It really was.

The doorbell rang a few moments later, so I grabbed my purse and went to the front door to greet Pete.

"She's as good as new!" Pete said.

"Well, she better be!" I replied. "Otherwise I am going to hold you personally responsible."

"I truly am sorry for the inconvenience," he apologized. "Would you like to drive or would you like me to?"

"You can," I responded. "I've had a pretty eventful morning, and I need to cool down a bit longer before I get behind the wheel."

"Oh? What happened?" he asked.

So, I told him all about this connection that seemed to exist between Sarah, Rosalie, and Joe. I still didn't know what to make of all of it, but I tell you, Pete seemed very interested in the whole ordeal. Why Pete should care was beyond me, but he definitely wanted to know more. There wasn't much more to tell him, though. All I knew was that Sarah was the woman standing next to Joe in the photograph, and that this also connected her to Rosalie. Well, in addition to finding Rosalie's number in Dianne's address book.

We arrived at the dealership, and Pete got out of the driver's seat and walked around to open my door for me. Not that I wasn't perfectly capable of doing it for myself, but I'm a sucker for a man who still knows how to act chivalrous. I got out of the passenger seat, and Pete literally wrapped his big arms around me in a warm and tender embrace. I was caught off guard.

"What was that for?" I asked, after I managed to untangle myself from his grasp.

"You just seemed like you needed a hug. That's all," he assured me.

"I suppose I did. How about another one?" I teased.

"You're a trip, Esther Kellerman. You know that? Taking care of not one but two women you barely even know. And you act like it's no big deal. And then there's the trading in of your Caddy for this Saab. I never would have guessed that when you walked into the showroom that day, what an incredible woman you are."

"Damn. If only I was thirty years younger. On second thought, how would your mother feel about you dating an older woman? A much older woman?" I asked, chuckling as I spoke.

"I think she'd say that older women just aren't my type," Pete replied.

"A pity," I offered. "Well, I'll be going now. Let me know when you hear back from that interview yesterday."

"I will," he said, as I walked around to the driver's-side door to get in and head on home.

On the way, I stopped off for a bite to eat at the club. They have a café on the pool side of the complex that's pretty casual, so I went in and ordered myself a burger and fries and a glass of water at the counter and then took a seat overlooking a nicely manicured courtyard. As I was waiting for my food, you'll never guess who walked in. Rosalie, that's who. Just the person I wanted to see. But as soon as she saw me she turned right around and walked back out.

"Rosalie," I yelled, but she either didn't hear me or didn't care.

I started to go after her, but the girl at the counter said my food was ready—so I had to make a decision between chasing after Rosalie and eating. Needless to say, I chose the latter. I went back up to the counter to retrieve my food and managed to eat a couple of the fries on my way back to my seat. They make the best fries here. Always fresh!

As I started on the burger, a thought occurred to me. The only reason Rosalie would have turned around and walked out after she saw me was that she didn't want to see me. But why didn't she want to see me? And did she know that I had wanted to see her? I started thinking about who I've talked to since discovering this connection, and the only two people I could think of are Pete and Phyllis. I highly doubted that Pete would have gone through the trouble of looking Rosalie up to dish to her. He didn't even know her! No, it had to be Phyllis.

So Phyllis and Rosalie are in cahoots, somehow. They've teamed up to keep something from me. Something about Sarah. For a brief moment, I wondered if Sarah is somehow Phyllis's real mother. But then I remembered the agonizing hours of labor I went through to give birth to her, so no. It couldn't be that. I'm pretty sure I'm Phyllis's biological mother. But it just goes to show you the leaps one's mind will make when confronted with some sort of secret being kept from you.

I finished my burger and fries and headed back out towards my car. But before I left the building, I picked up the phone in the lobby area and called Rosalie. No answer. I then called Phyllis. No answer. Damn. When I get my hands on the two of them, they're surely going to be in a world of hurt.

My car started right up, and I headed towards home. But as I pulled into the neighborhood, I had a better idea. I decided to stop by Sarah's house to speak to Dianne. You see, it had suddenly occurred to me that the fact that these people moved into our neighborhood who clearly have a connection to my family was a pretty big coincidence. Too big, if you ask me.

I pulled into their driveway, got out, and walked around to the front door to ring the bell. No one answered immediately, so I rang the bell again. Eventually, Sarah came to the door and let me in. At least she remembered that she knew me this time. I asked her where Dianne was, but she didn't know who I was talking about.

"Dianne!" I yelled as I walked into the living room.

There was no answer from anywhere in the house. Sarah looked at me and asked who Dianne was.

"Oh, for heaven's sake, Sarah! I don't have time for this. Just

The Enlightenment of Esther

please go and sit down on the sofa for me. I can't believe she left you here all by yourself."

Sarah looked at me blankly.

"Go! Sit!" I shouted and pointed towards the sofa. She did as she was told.

I went and searched the rest of the house, but Dianne was nowhere to be found. I opened the door to the garage, but Dianne's car was gone. Damn. She really did leave. I walked back into the house and started pacing, trying to figure out what to do next. I picked up the phone and tried both Rosalie and Phyllis. There was no answer at either residence. Fishing through my purse, I retrieved my address book and looked up David's work number since I still didn't have it memorized.

David's secretary answered the phone and said that he was unavailable but that I could leave a message for him if I wished.

"Yes, I would very much like to leave him a message. Tell him that Esther Kellerman called and that she is on a tear. Tell him that she's had just about enough of dealing with his mother and his wife, and that if he wants to ensure that they are both still alive when he gets home, that he should leave his office with all due speed!"

Yes, I know what you're about to say. You think I should have dialed down the drama a bit. You think I'm overreacting. Well, let me tell you something. You don't know what overreacting is until you've seen Esther Kellerman launch into orbit! I have half a mind to just walk out of here this very instant. The only thing stopping me from doing so is poor Sarah, who really shouldn't be left alone.

So, I resigned myself to taking a seat next to Sarah on the sofa. She patted my hand and said that everything was going to be okay.

"Who were you talking to on the phone?" she asked.

"Your son's secretary," I answered.

"My son's secretary? He's only ten. Too young to have a secretary. Unless he's turned one of the girls at school into one," she laughed.

Even I had to laugh at this. I decided to play along this time.

"Does your son have a lot of friends?" I asked.

"Oh yes, he's a very popular child. And very smart too. He's good with numbers. Just like his father."

"His father? What does his father do for a living?" I asked.

"You can ask him yourself. He just ran out to the store for some eggs. He'll be back soon."

And we were back to that again. She thinks he's still alive and coming home soon with eggs. Interesting, though. She didn't answer my question. I thought about pressing her on this, but I figured I'd better count my lucky stars that she doesn't think I'm trying to take him away from her again.

Just then, I heard the garage door opening. A minute later, Dianne was back in the kitchen with a carton of eggs in her hand. Well, at least Sarah got something right. A warm body with a carton of eggs did in fact return.

"Esther," she said in mock surprise, as she had clearly seen my car in the driveway.

Well, I laid into her like there was no tomorrow. She tried to explain that Sarah was insistent on having an omelet and that they were out of eggs. I told her that that was no excuse for leaving Sarah unattended. She sheepishly backed down.

"Sit," I said to Dianne while pointing at the kitchen table.

She sat down. I took the seat next to hers.

"I returned to speak with you about Sarah and her connection to my late husband, Joe, and his sister Rosalie," I said and waited to gauge her response.

"Esther," Dianne began while grasping my hand, "how

much do you know about your late husband's life before you met him?"

"What do you mean?" I asked her, slightly confused.

"I mean, from the time he left his mother's house to the time he married you. What do you know?"

"Well, he went off to college and then started working as an accountant. I know he had a few girlfriends along the way. Whether Sarah was one of them, I do not know. But I know that she was very familiar with the Kellerman family."

"If you don't mind my asking, how did you make the connection?"

"Never you mind that, dear. The important thing is that I do know. I'm pretty sure it's no coincidence that you all moved into this particular neighborhood."

"Well," she started to say when the phone rang. Damn.

It was Muriel on the phone. She wanted to speak to me, so I walked over to the phone and took the receiver from Dianne.

"Hello, dear," I began. "How are you feeling? Any better?"

"Oh yes. Definitely better than this morning. I'll be back there with you tomorrow for our last day."

"Glad to hear it," I responded. "Anything else?"

She said no, so I hung up the phone. I wanted to get back to my interrogation of Dianne, but the damn phone rang again. This time it was David. Apparently, he had gotten my message and was calling to inquire about the situation here. Dianne assured him that she had it under control and that he didn't need to leave work.

"Give me the phone," I said to Dianne as I motioned towards the receiver.

She handed it to me, and I started in on him, too. I asked him point blank how his mother was connected to my late husband. He said he wasn't sure he should be the one to tell me. I asked him who then. He told me to talk to my daughter.

So, I was right. My daughter Phyllis is in cahoots with these people. I hung up the phone, grabbed my purse, and walked straight out of their house for the second time today.

23

Instead of driving straight over to Phyllis's to confront her, which is probably what you expected I would do, I went straight home. I figured I had had enough human contact for one day, and all I wanted at this point was to be alone. The two women whom I am closest to, Phyllis and Rosalie, have both betrayed me. Well, to hell with them.

I walked back into my house after pulling into the garage and headed straight for the bookshelves containing all of my photo albums. It took me awhile to find what I was looking for, since I couldn't remember which album it was in. But I finally found it: Joe and Rosalie's mother's wedding photo. A copy of the same photograph Rosalie showed me yesterday. But upon closer inspection, I realized that there was indeed a difference. In my version of the photograph, there is no unidentified woman standing next to Joe. He's on the right side of the photo, and then the photo ends.

Then I looked a little more closely, and I realized that the right edge of the photograph was a little uneven. I don't know how I never noticed this before, but it was definitely uneven. Joe must have cut this woman, who I am now sure is Sarah, out of the picture. If Joe and Sarah were in a relationship, they must have had a pretty bad breakup for him to just completely cut her out.

I started reminiscing a bit on the past. When I first met Joe, I remember him telling me that he had been through a bad breakup not long before then. At the time, I chose not to ask him about the details of the breakup, and to tell you the truth, I really hadn't thought about it much since. Joe and I had such a connection and such mutual attraction that it seemed like that whatever had happened in our respective pasts didn't matter anymore. Not that I had much of a past myself, but you get the gist. It was almost as if both of our lives had started at the very moment we met.

It was the height of the Depression when we met, and everyone I knew was either out of work completely or just getting by on what part-time jobs they could find. I was already in my twenties at this point and was trying to find work myself. My father had passed, so we were in real dire straits financially. I took in whatever sewing work I could, as did my mother and two sisters. But it wasn't enough to sustain us. Not really.

So, I started looking for any type of stable employment I could find. And this is what led to me meeting Joe. I managed to land a job as a cigarette girl at a local burlesque theater, and one night, Joe walked in with some of his buddies. Like I said before, he had had a bad breakup, and his buddies thought that seeing a burlesque show would get his mind off of his broken heart. As I walked by the table where he and his buddies were sitting, he stopped me and asked for a pack. I sold one to him, and he gave me a very nice tip.

A few minutes later, I was making my way back towards his

The Enlightenment of Esther

side of the theater. He flagged me down and asked for another pack. So I sold him another pack, and he gave me another nice tip. Well, this went on for a while, and before I knew it, I was completely out of packs of cigarettes. He had them all stacked up in front of him on the table. I asked him if he was going to smoke all of those cigarettes himself, but he told me he didn't smoke.

I then asked him if he had a pen I could borrow, which he did. Pulling out one of the many dollar bills that he had been giving me all night, I wrote my first name and phone number down on it. He looked down at the dollar bill and then gave me a wink.

And then I said, "Since you're not going to smoke those cigarettes, mind if I take them back and sell them to those who will?"

I figured I could pocket the funds from reselling them, and I really desperately needed the money. No one could ever accuse me of lacking in entrepreneurial skills! He gave me a wry smile and gestured for me to take the packs back, which I did as quickly as I could, not wanting him to change his mind.

At the end of the show, Joe and his buddies got up to leave, but before they could make their way to the exit, I stopped him and laid one on him. Right there, in public. To this day, I don't know what made me do it, but I just had a really good feeling about him. Was it love at first sight? Probably not, but I was definitely interested and I wanted him to know it.

He called me the next day and asked if I'd consider accompanying him to dinner that evening. I told him I had to work again, but that I'd be free afterwards for a drink. Prohibition had ended the year before, and though I was a bit wary of meeting a man for a drink, it was the only way I could think of to see him that night. But I made him promise not to come to the show again and buy up all of my cigarettes! He suggested a place near the theater, and we agreed to meet there around nine o'clock.

I was running a few minutes late, but he was there waiting patiently for me when I arrived. He ordered a scotch and asked me what I wanted to drink. Since I really didn't have much experience with alcohol, I asked for the same. Those first few sips went down like fire, but then I started to actually enjoy it. This was the beginning of a lifelong love affair for me with scotch, and Joe and I would often have a glass in the evenings throughout our marriage.

If you were to ask me what we talked about that night, I'd have a hard time telling you since I really don't remember myself. What I do remember from that night was staring into his beautiful, kind eyes and knowing that this was the man I was going to marry someday. We must have talked for hours because I didn't get home until well after midnight. I found my mother waiting up for me when I walked in the door, and of course, she started interrogating me. She asked me what kind of a boy keeps a girl out past a decent hour. I told her the kind of boy who knew a good thing when he saw one!

Joe and I started dating, and after three weeks, he proposed. Totally out of the blue. My first instinct was to say yes and ride him all the way to the altar, but I hesitated. That his previous relationship had ended not long before really concerned me. I didn't want to get hurt if it turned out I was really just a rebound for him. He looked at me perplexedly when I didn't give him an answer.

I ended up telling him that I'd give him an answer soon, but that I wasn't quite ready to say yes. I had never heard of anyone asking someone to marry them after only three weeks of dating. It just wasn't done. When I told my mother that Joe had proposed, she went into orbit, asking me what kind of man would do such a foolish thing. She wisely said that when you marry someone, you marry their family too, and he hadn't even met her or my sisters for that matter. You see, he'd pick me up from our house and I'd run to meet him at the curb. So the only glimpse my mother and sisters ever got of him was from watching him open the car door for me.

A few days after the proposal, I asked Joe to come and meet my family. I promised him that if he still wanted to marry me after meeting them, and if my mother gave her blessing, I would say yes. Well, my mother didn't make the best impression on him. She tried every trick in her book to discourage him from wanting to marry me. She told him she thought he could do better. She told him that I was pretty plain to look at. She told him I was opinionated and that he'd never have a peaceful night again if he married me. But her pièce de résistance was telling him that I wasn't a virgin. How my mother knew I wasn't a virgin I'll never know.

I walked Joe to the door and told him to wait around and that I'd be out in a moment. As soon as I closed the door behind him, my mother turned to me and told me we had her blessing. I loved my mother dearly, but sometimes she drove me to distraction. I asked her why she said all of those things to him, to which she replied that she wanted to see if he would still love me when he realized that I wasn't perfect. I gave her a big hug and then ran out the door after Joe. Before he could get in a word, I said yes.

We were married six months later in a traditional Jewish ceremony under the chuppah. The rabbi was a bit bellicose for my tastes but he was a family friend to Joe and his family, so I didn't put up a fuss. The wedding was in the sanctuary of Joe's synagogue, and the reception was held in an adjacent party hall. It was a small affair, just family and close friends. My youngest sister was my maid of honor, and Joe's childhood friend was his best man. Since both of our fathers had already passed and neither one of us had any brothers, my mother gave me away. Our honeymoon consisted of a drive up to Lake Erie for a few days, staying in a secluded rental cabin.

When I think back upon those early years, they fill me with joy. But that all ended when America entered the war. Joe was drafted into the navy and ended up in the Battle of Guadalcanal. He would never talk about it after the war ended, and I never really asked. It's been my experience that there are vets who love regaling others in their war stories, and then there are vets who refuse to talk about the war at all.

The years after the war were good years. Prosperous years. Joe's accounting firm was thriving. Phyllis was blossoming into a beautiful young girl. I learned how to play bridge and even competed in tournaments once Phyllis was past the point of needing me at home.

As the years passed, Joe and I began to travel more. We eventually started traveling to countries that no Jew dared go after the war. We even went to Germany, if you can believe that. In between trips, though, I would spend time helping Rosalie with her husband, and then her lover, as their dementia progressed. I mean, she still did most of the caretaking, but I'd go over now and then and give her a day off.

I suppose what I am trying to say is that my life before I met Joe paled in comparison to my life with him. I never really asked him much about his past relationships. And since he never brought them up in conversation, I never saw a reason to ask. It would seem now that I was foolish not to, as I might otherwise now have a better idea of who exactly Sarah is.

Interrupting my train of thought, the phone rang, so I got

up from where I was sitting to answer it. A voice I didn't recognize was on the other end. She asked me if this was the Kellerman residence, to which I answered that it was. She then told me to hold on for a second so that she could hand the phone over to someone who wanted to talk to me.

"Esther," a weakened voice said.

"Lilia? Is that you?" I asked, pretty certain that it was.

"Yes," she responded. "Her last name."

"What? Who? What are you talking about, Lilia?" I asked, a bit confused. Not that this was anything new for me lately.

"The woman."

"What woman?"

"You look after," she said.

"Oh, you mean Sarah?" I asked, my head starting to clear a bit. "Her last name is Locker. Remember? I'm pretty sure I mentioned her last name to you yesterday when we were at the doctor's office."

"Married name?"

"What?" I asked.

"Or maiden name?"

"Married name, I presume. David and Dianne have the same last name, so I'm pretty sure it came from David's late father."

"Sure?" she asked.

"I have no reason not to be. What are you getting at, Lilia?"

"Maybe two Sarah Lockers. One I knew. One you know."

"It's certainly possible. Neither Sarah nor Locker are uncommon names."

The line went dead. I don't know what's gotten into everyone lately. All I know is that I was trying to put together a puzzle, and someone was deliberately keeping some of the pieces from me.

24

Muriel called the next morning and said she was heading over to Sarah's, and that I should take my time and how appreciative she was of me taking over yesterday. I thanked her and hung up the phone, as I wasn't quite sure if I really wanted to go into all the details with her regarding what actually happened yesterday.

So I spent a leisurely early morning drinking my coffee, eating a couple of croissants and reading the newspaper. There was an article about North Dakota and South Dakota celebrating their one hundredth birthdays yesterday. Boring. Then I saw a headline for an article about Columbus mayor Buck Rinehart. I skipped that one. Finally, I landed on a piece about elder care and the looming crisis. I read on a bit, but it hit a little too close to home for me.

Next I flipped on the television and watched some morning news, and then watched some more morning news. I was bored. I'm not so sure this working girl is ready for retirement just yet. Seems like I've been running a mile a minute since the beginning of last month and haven't really had much of a break. But now that I have one this morning, it was like I didn't know what to do with myself. Maybe I should get a job in a nursing home or something. Especially since I'm no longer speaking to Phyllis or Rosalie.

At around 10 a.m., I arrived at Sarah's for what would be my last shift. I knocked on the door and waited for Muriel to answer, but she didn't come. So I knocked again and rang the bell. Eventually, Sarah answered the door and invited me in. She told me to be very quiet because there was an old lady who was fast asleep on the couch and she didn't want me to disturb her. How thoughtful of Sarah.

"How long has she been asleep?" I whispered to Sarah.

"Oh, I don't know. Maybe a couple of days," Sarah responded.

"I doubt it's really been a couple of days, dear. She'd be dead," I said.

Sarah's eyes widened, so I reassured her that Muriel hadn't been here more than a couple of hours. This seemed to put her at ease.

"So, what would you like to do today? Would you like for me to read a book to you? Or maybe we could try putting a puzzle together. Wouldn't that be fun?" I asked.

"I don't want to disturb the old lady there on the couch, so let's try a puzzle."

"Okay. Do you know if there are any puzzles in the house?" I asked her.

"I don't know. Do you?"

"No, dear. That's why I asked you," I replied. "Never mind, I'll see if I can find one somewhere around here."

So I went off in search of a puzzle. I was hoping maybe there would be one in the hall closet near the front door, but there weren't any. I did find some board games, though. I started sifting through them, but I wasn't having much luck finding something that I thought she'd be able to handle. Monopoly was too strategic. Risk took too long to play. There were sets of checkers and chess, but again, too strategic. I needed to find something that was based purely on luck. Something with dice.

The next game I came across had a rather, um, risqué name. It was called Passion or Poison. I read the details on the cover, which I wish I hadn't, but basically, it's a game that tests your knowledge of your spouse's desires. Needless to say, I had no interest in discovering Sarah's desires, nor did I want her asking me about mine. I put the game away, though to tell you the truth, I had half a mind to just throw it in the trash.

There was a Yahtzee set, but the rules were probably too complicated for Sarah to remember. Finally, I saw a game I remember playing with my granddaughters: Sorry. I was thinking this might be simple enough for Sarah to manage, with a little help from me. Hell, I'll probably just let her win, since who knows what kind of behavior a defeat for her would spark. A victory might keep her in a good mood for the rest of the day!

"Sarah," I said as I carried the game back to the kitchen table. "I couldn't find any puzzles, but look what I did find! Have you ever played this before? It's called Sorry."

She shook her head.

"Well, it's a really fun game and really easy to learn. Want to give it a shot?" I asked.

She nodded.

"Okay, let me set it up, and I'll go over the rules with you. What color do you want to be? You can be Red, Yellow, Green, or Blue."

"Blue. Blue is my favorite color. Did you know that? I have this pretty blue dress that sometimes I get to wear to school. On special days."

At least she's in the right mind-set for playing a children's board game! I decided to just count my blessings and not mention to her that she's about seventy-five years too old to be wearing a pretty blue dress to school for special occasions.

I set up the game and chose Red as my color since it matches my new but slightly lemony new car. I put my pieces in the red starting circle and put Sarah's blue pieces in the blue starting circle. I then tried to explain as succinctly as I could the rules of the game. She seemed to be following what I was saying, but there was no way to tell for sure until we started playing.

"Okay, Sarah. You go first. Pick a card from the pile and flip it over," I said.

The card she picked had the number 6 on it. I waited to see if she would know what to do, but she didn't. So I instructed her to take one of her pieces from the starting circle and move it six spaces on the board in a clockwise direction. She didn't know what I meant by "clockwise," so I told her that I really meant to say "left." This she understood and moved her piece accordingly.

I then drew the number 8, and I moved one of my pieces from the starting circle. We went through taking turns, but she wasn't getting it. I was pretty much playing against myself. Well, it was worth a try, and Sarah seemed to be enjoying it, so we continued on until all of our pieces were out of the starting circle and well on their way to the finish line. She got a little upset, though, when one of my pieces landed on the same space one of hers was occupying, and I had to explain to her that her piece had to go back to the starting circle as a result. I assured her that she would be able to get that piece back on the board on her next turn, and that seemed to calm her down.

We were just about done with the game when Sarah stood up unexpectedly and walked away. She was heading towards Muriel, so it was all I could do to get out of my seat and stop her. Muriel seemed to be sleeping so peacefully, and I didn't want Sarah to disturb her. Without much thought to it, I gently clapped my hands together to try to get Sarah's attention, and thankfully, it worked. She turned around and headed back towards the kitchen table.

"Shhh! Don't clap. You'll wake the old lady on the couch," Sarah admonished me.

"Well, it looked like you were going over there to wake her up. I had to stop you," I shot back.

"I wanted to make sure she's still breathing," Sarah responded.

"She's not dead, Sarah. She's just napping because you wore her out this morning, and she isn't feeling well."

"What's wrong with her?" Sarah asked.

"How should I know? Nobody tells me anything anymore. It's like the whole world has conspired against me to keep me in the dark. And that includes you and your son and your daughter-in-law."

I was definitely raising my voice by this point, so I stopped and tried to get a hold of myself. Plus, I could see that Sarah had no idea what I was talking about.

"Sarah," I began. "Let's sit back down and talk quietly for a bit. I have an idea. Since I couldn't find an actual puzzle earlier, how about we play a puzzle with words? Would that be okay?"

Sarah looked a bit apprehensive, but she sat back down at the table.

"How do you play?" she asked.

The Enlightenment of Esther

"Well, that's a good question," I responded. "Why don't we start by playing the Geography game. Have you ever played?"

"No."

I explained the rules to her, and we started to play. We had a couple of successful rounds, but then she got stuck when I said Halifax. She couldn't come up with a place that started with X, so that pretty much ended the game. Yes, I know it was rather rude of me to give her such a difficult letter, but I had an ulterior motive. I needed to get her comfortable with playing a word game first before I got to what I was really aiming for.

"Okay, let's try another game," I suggested. "I promise you'll really like this one. And you'll be good at it, too."

She smiled and nodded.

"So, this game is really simple. I am going to say a word or a phrase, and all you have to do is say the first thing that comes to your mind. Understand?"

She nodded. I wasn't sure if this was really a good idea, but I needed to find a way to get inside her mind, and my thought was that by turning this into a simple reflexive game, she'd be more cooperative.

"Are you ready? The first word is 'mother.'"

"'Father,'" she responded.

"That's right!" I said. "Good job!"

We went through a few more of these, and she seemed to be doing okay. So then I laid it all out on the table. I said, "Maiden name."

She looked at me blankly. I wanted to know what her maiden name was. Was it Locker? Or was that indeed her married name? These were questions that I felt only she would answer truthfully. There was no way I was going to trust David or Dianne at this point to level with me. They hid from me the connection between Sarah, Joe, and Rosalie, so I was pretty sure if I asked them anything about Sarah's past, they either wouldn't cooperate or they'd lie to me.

But Sarah didn't seem to comprehend what I was asking her. I tried asking her some more questions about her past, specifically about her parents, but she was coming up empty. There wasn't much I could do at this point, so I gave up.

"What would you like for lunch, dear?" I asked Sarah.

"Oh, I don't know. Whatever," she responded.

I went into the kitchen and rummaged through the fridge, seeing what I could make for her. It was slim pickings, though. I'd have to speak to David and Dianne about keeping this house better stocked with food. Even though today was my last day here, I'd hate for whoever is going to take over to find themselves in such a pickle. And speaking of pickles, I was really craving one, but there wasn't a pickle in sight.

"How about a grilled cheese sandwich?" I asked.

"With tomato soup?" she requested.

I looked in the pantry and thankfully found a couple of cans of tomato soup, so I figured we'd all have grilled cheese sandwiches and tomato soup. I wasn't about to make three separate meals for us. Sarah asked if I needed any help, but I told her not worry about it and that I had it covered.

About ten minutes later, I had the soup heated up and the grilled cheese sandwiches cooked to perfection, if I do say so myself. I ladled the soup into three white porcelain bowls and took two of them over to the table. I then took the third bowl and one grilled cheese sandwich over and made a final trip for the remaining sandwiches. I asked Sarah what she wanted to drink. No response. So I filled three glasses of water from the tap and started to bring them to the table, but one of them slipped out of my hands and spilled on the floor.

Well, shit. Water was all over the place, and I'd have to go find some towels to mop it all up. I yelled at Muriel to wake up and help me with this mess, but she didn't stir. Sarah shushed me, but I paid no attention to her. I walked myself over to where Muriel was sitting and started yelling again. She still didn't stir.

I reached for her hand, but when my skin made contact with hers, something wasn't right. I grabbed on to her shoulders to shake her a bit. Nothing. I turned her wrist over to find her pulse, but there was no pulse to be found.

25

According to the doctors, Muriel died of a heart attack. They say that it was probably an instantaneous death and that she most likely felt no pain at all. I suppose that's a blessing of some sort, but I found it of little comfort. It's not as if Muriel was the first of my friends to pass away over the years, but she was certainly the closest. Her death brought my own mortality to the forefront of my mind, and I just can't shake this cloud of despair that's been hovering over me these last two days.

Her funeral is set for tomorrow, and her daughters, their husbands, and their children have all flown in for it. I had called the eldest daughter about an hour after Muriel's death to let her know that their mother had passed away, and let me tell you, it's a phone call I hope never to have to make again. The tortured anguish in her voice after I broke the news was almost more than I could bear. Mercifully, she said she'd call her sister for me, so at least I didn't have to tell another daughter that her mother was dead.

When I realized Muriel had no pulse, I called the paramedics, and then I called both David and Dianne to let them know they needed to return home as soon as was possible. I still don't know how long Muriel had been sitting on that sofa without an ounce of life in her body, but whatever the length, the paramedics could tell that there was no chance of reviving her. I asked them if they could wait a few minutes while I called our rabbi to see if he could come over and say a prayer. Not the Mourner's Kaddish, but I can't remember the name of it now. It's more of an immediate prayer in our faith when someone dies.

Fortunately, our rabbi was free and able to come over quickly. If it had been a few hours later, he would have been too busy preparing for Friday evening services. The paramedics patiently waited, as one of them was also Jewish and insisted on doing so. Once the rabbi was done, they asked me to take Sarah into another room while they did what they needed to do to transport her to the morgue until we could arrange to have her body delivered to wherever the funeral was to be held.

One of the paramedics asked about cremation, but I said no. It's not our way. I probably should have checked with Muriel's daughters about that. Oh well. If they want her cremated later, they can still do so. Whereas if I had arranged for her to be cremated, and then her daughters said they wanted her buried in full, it would have been too late.

I didn't really know exactly where I should take Sarah since her house's living spaces are more of an open concept. We ended up going into her bedroom and sat next to each other on the bed. I asked her if she knew what was going on. She said she did, but I wasn't so sure. So I asked her more specifically if she understood that Muriel had passed away. She nodded and then started to tear up. I'd like to believe that even if she couldn't remember Muriel's name most days, she knew Muriel had been a part of her life in some capacity.

There was a box of tissues sitting on Sarah's nightstand, so I grabbed a few for both of us. I tried to be stoic about it, for Sarah's sake, but I just couldn't manage it. I started sobbing, and there was no stopping it. Sarah looked concerned and tried to comfort me. I suppose that even in the throes of a vicious disease like dementia, you never really lose your capacity for empathy. Well, unless you never had it to begin with, I suppose.

We just sat there for what seemed like an eternity, waiting for the paramedics to finish what they needed to do. Sarah asked me if I thought Muriel would go to heaven, and I told her that we Jews pretty much believe everyone does. She seemed comforted by that, and I reassured her that she too would go to heaven one day, even if she wasn't Jewish. This elicited a mixed response from her—first laughter and then a more pensive reaction. I asked her what was wrong, but she couldn't seem to find her words again, so I just put my hand on her back and rubbed for a while.

The paramedics came in a few moments later and said we could come back out. They were just leaving when David burst into the house and ran to Sarah. He put his arms around her and wouldn't let go, a really touching and tender moment. I kind of felt like I was intruding on them, to be honest. David was probably wrestling with his own mother's mortality, just as I was beginning to wrestle with mine. I took my leave of them and told David I'd be in touch regarding the funeral arrangements once they were made.

I had called Muriel's eldest daughter when I returned home, and I just about collapsed on my bed from exhaustion afterwards, both physically and emotionally. My dear friend was dead, and all because she overworked herself to try to protect her late husband's name. And then there was Pete, and all of my anger towards him that had dissipated over the last month resurfaced with a vengeance. That he was blackmailing Muriel for money to take care of his own mother Lilia was incredibly galling to me.

And to make matters worse, I told Muriel's eldest daughter that I'd help with the funeral arrangements since I was local and she and her sister were not. By the end of the conversation I had a pretty good feeling that I'd be making most of the arrangements myself, though I did ask her to write an obituary to be placed in the *Columbus Dispatch*. She'd be able to fax it over to them when she was done. Plus, it'd give her the opportunity to pay for it, since the cost really should be on her and her sister. I'm not running a bank printing free money, you know!

I woke up a few hours later after a much-needed nap and set myself to the task of calling Muriel's friends and acquaintances in the area, at least the ones whom I knew about. I called all of the ladies in our book club, save for Rosalie. Since she didn't seem to want to talk to me, I figured someone else from the club would spill the beans to her. I called the ladies from our bridge game at the club next, and after I was done with those, I called a few other friends in the neighborhood to let them know.

Fortunately, I had actually already arranged with the rabbi a date and time for the funeral, and he offered to call the funeral home and make arrangements for Muriel's body to be transferred there. I just had to call the cemetery to let them know that we would be depositing Muriel with them via a graveside service on Monday after we were done at the funeral home. Unfortunately, it was already after 5 p.m. when I tried to call them, so no one answered. They did have an answering machine, so I left what details I could regarding the timing for Muriel's burial. If we show up and they're not ready for us, oh well. We're not taking her back.

Once I was completely done making calls, I walked back into my bedroom and headed for the closet. I needed to figure out what I was going to wear, and to be honest, I wasn't sure that anything I had was going to fit right. I've lost a few pounds of my own over the last month. Maybe not enough to make a difference, but you never know. There was a new dark gray double-breasted skirt suit that I hadn't yet had a chance to wear. It was still in the dry-cleaning bag from when I had it cleaned after I purchased it. But what to wear underneath? A blouse? A turtleneck? Or maybe nothing but a bra and give everyone a good show! In the end, I settled on a silky cream-colored crew-cut shirt. Simple and elegant.

I spent the last two days selecting and ordering flowers and putting together the shiva for after the burial. I called Muriel's eldest daughter yesterday to see if she wanted to have the shiva at her mother's house or if she'd prefer for me to host it here in my home. She said she'd really appreciate it if we could do the shiva at my house, so I told her it'd be fine and that I'd take care of the details. Unlike five years ago when Joe passed away, I made sure not only to prepay for the food, I made absolutely sure I gave the right date and time for delivery. I wasn't about to screw up another shiva!

But making all of the arrangements was really just putting a bandage on the hurt and anguish I was feeling. Muriel's death was certainly a big part of it, but it's been two days since her death, and I still hadn't heard a peep out of Rosalie or Phyllis. I was sure that both of them knew about it by now, but whatever secrets they were keeping from me regarding Sarah were obviously more important than reaching out to me in my

The Enlightenment of Esther

time of need. Well, to hell with them. To hell with the both of them.

I called Pete to tell him about Muriel's passing. I gave him the details for the funeral and the shiva and told him that both he and Lilia should come. I also called David and told him the three of them should attend as well as I thought it was important for Sarah to get some sense of understanding and closure regarding Muriel's death. Finally, I called Richard, our hair stylist, to tell him as well. I figured if his book wasn't too busy tomorrow, he'd be able to come for either the funeral or the shiva. Did I invite all of these people purely out of spite against Rosalie? Well, maybe a little, but they all had a connection to Muriel, and it seemed to me that they might want the opportunity to say good-bye.

With nothing left to do, I decided to head over to the club for dinner by myself. I suppose I could have invited someone from the bridge club or the book club to join me, but the idea of making small talk with anyone right now wasn't very appealing. So I hopped in my car and headed out for dinner.

After handing the keys off to the valet, I walked in and was greeted by Walter, looking handsome as ever. He looked around me, probably wondering if Rosalie was just behind. When I told him it was just me tonight, he asked me if I wanted my usual table or if I might consider sitting at the bar and eating there instead. There was another room in the main building that was named after some golf pro whose name I don't recall, but in terms of atmosphere, the room was somewhere in between the casual poolside café and the fancier main dining room we usually eat in for dinner.

I decided to try out the bar, as Walter had suggested. It wasn't exactly my favorite room in the Club, but I thought a change in scenery would do me some good. And I couldn't even remember the last time I actually sat at a bar on a stool. I was just grateful to be wearing pants so that I wouldn't have to deal with getting on and off the stool in a skirt. Believe me, it wouldn't have been a pretty sight.

The bartender was a nice young man named Tripp, whom I had never met. Blond hair, blue eyes, and definitely a gentile. He looked to be about the same age as my middle granddaughter. I wonder if they might even know each other. Perhaps they were even in school together. I'd have to remember to mention him to her when she's home in a few weeks for Thanksgiving.

Once I was planted on the stool, I asked Tripp for a scotch and a menu. While he was pouring my drink, I perused the selection of entrees for the evening, but nothing seemed very appetizing. There was a halibut dish on special, served with a chutney that didn't sound too appealing. None of the regular items on the menu, and believe me I've had all of them a million times, piqued my taste buds either. Then a thought occurred to me. I asked Tripp if there were any secret dishes not on the menu that the chefs would prepare on request. I had never thought to ask this before, but I figured I had nothing to lose.

Tripp said that the chefs make a really good shrimp scampi upon request. I told him I was Jewish and didn't eat shrimp. He looked at me skeptically. I asked him which part of my statement he didn't believe. He said that most of the Jewish people he knows either secretly or openly eat shrimp. Well, he had me. I've been known to put away a shrimp cocktail or two in my lifetime, and since I wasn't eating with Rosalie tonight, I said why not and ordered the shrimp scampi.

The bar was pretty empty tonight, so I had a chance to converse with Tripp for a bit. I think he could tell that I had a lot on my mind and needed someone to talk to. I tell you, I felt like I was in an episode of *Cheers*, just pouring my soul out to this bartender. He listened patiently and offered me a napkin when I started to tear up a bit. And then before I knew it, I was sobbing my eyes out. He came around the bar to my side and gently hugged me and told me that everything would work out one way or another. He said he believes that everything happens for a reason, even if we don't always know what the reason is at the time.

And then it hit me. I totally forgot! Muriel's eldest daughter had called back earlier this morning to ask if I would give the eulogy at the funeral tomorrow. I was in such a rush to get her off the phone that I said "sure" before even giving it a second thought. Well, let me tell you, I'm definitely having second thoughts now! Oh, dear. What was I going to do? In my nearly eighty years on this good earth, I've never given a eulogy. Not even at my own parents' funerals.

Tripp was looking at me with concern now, so I went ahead and told him about me agreeing to give the eulogy tomorrow. He thought it was a bit odd that the family wouldn't choose someone from within their own ranks for this, umm, honor. But I knew Muriel, and I knew her daughters. The fact that her daughters and their families had planned to celebrate Thanksgiving in the Bahamas this year should tell you all you need to know about the nature of their relationship to Muriel. While I have no knowledge of any animus among the family, they were not close.

He asked me what I was going to say about Muriel, so I had to tell him that I had completely forgotten about the eulogy until just a moment ago. He told me to hold that thought while he went back into the kitchen to see if my shrimp scampi was ready, so I started running through the various clichés one often uses in eulogies. "She was a devoted mother, wife, daughter, etc.," or "She was a pillar of her community."

My personal favorite, though, is, "She was the kindest woman and didn't have mean bone in her body." What a bunch of crap! Everyone has a mean bone in their body, whether they admit it or not! And don't you just love how people's memories of those who have passed away become rosier and rosier as the years progress? You remember how Nixon visited President Reagan last year in the White House? Ten years ago, he wouldn't have been allowed anywhere near the premises! And now, he's an invited guest! He isn't even dead yet, and people's perceptions of him are softening.

Interrupting my train of thought, Tripp returned with my hot bowl of shrimp scampi. I dug in like there was no tomorrow! He laughed and told me to slow down or I'd make myself sick. We talked a bit about the eulogy, and he gave me some good suggestions, having had to give the eulogy at his grandmother's funeral a few months ago. I asked him to write some of it down so that I could ponder over what he was saying. He went into some back room somewhere and returned with a pen and pad.

I finished up my dinner while Tripp wrote down some of what he had just said. He handed the pad to me, and I looked over what he wrote down, making sure there was nothing important missing. When I was satisfied, I tore off the top sheet, folded it, and put it in my purse. Tripp asked me if I would like some coffee and dessert, so I ordered some decaf and a scoop of that delicious raspberry chocolate chunk ice cream.

As he was handing me my coffee and ice cream, a thought occurred to me. I asked him what his plans were for tomorrow. He said tomorrow would be his first day off in two weeks. Well, I probably shouldn't have, but I asked him if he'd be interested in being my date for the funeral. Every head in that funeral home would turn when I walked in on the arms of a much younger man, and that satisfaction might just give me the confidence I needed to give this damned eulogy. And to my extreme surprise, he actually said yes and said it'd be an honor. Oh, what a mensch! But then I thought better of it and told him he was sweet to accept, but that I'd better go by myself.

26

Someone once said to me that you only learn the secret to life when you reach its end. This was the thought that was on my mind as I woke up this morning to get ready for the funeral and burial. I suppose Muriel knows this secret now, wherever she is. As for me, I'm nearly eighty years old, and these last few weeks have shown me how much I still have to learn. Not just about life itself but about the people I am surrounded by.

    I called Phyllis yesterday evening to make sure she and Bernie had the details for the funeral and burial, but no one answered, so I left a very curt message on the answering machine and asked her to pass along the information to her coconspirator, Rosalie. Well, Phyllis called back this morning just as I was sitting down for breakfast to ask if I wanted to ride with them to the service and the burial afterwards. I told her that I was perfectly capable of driving myself and that I would see them there. She hung up.

    After I got home from dinner last night, I wrote down exactly what I was going to say during my eulogy of Muriel, but

The Enlightenment of Esther

sitting here now drinking my coffee, I decided to make a few minor edits. This is going to be the eulogy to end all eulogies, and I fully intend to lay low all those present who don't measure up to the standards that Muriel lived her life by. She was a kind, caring, considerate, and generous woman, if a bit naïve. Oh, I'll leave her naïveté out of the speech, of course. Don't you worry. Muriel will be exalted onto the highest pedestal that my words can construct for her. And by the time I'm through, everyone at the service will be calling her one of God's true angels.

I finished making my edits and laid the multiple sheets of paper on the countertop near my purse so that I wouldn't forget them on my way out later. I was getting ready to take a shower when the phone rang, but I decided not to rush back to answer it. Anyone who was calling me now I'd probably see in a few hours anyway. And if it was Rosalie calling, I really had no desire to talk to her. You're probably wondering how I was planning to get through this ordeal without biting Rosalie's head off. Well, to be honest, I had no plan. I was just praying that my grief over Muriel's death would outweigh my anger towards Rosalie. And Phyllis, too. I give it a 50/50 chance of success.

As I was undressing to get into the shower, a thought occurred to me. You know how sometimes people will write on the back of a photograph the names of those who are in the picture?

I put my robe back on and went back into the living room where the photo albums were and quickly found the album containing the chopped off version of Joe's mother's second wedding family photo. I don't think I've ever looked at the back of the pictures in this album, but as they say, there's no time like the present. So I flipped through the album again until I found the photo I was looking for. Once I found it, I removed it from the page and flipped the image over to see if any identifying information was on the back.

What I probably should have thought of, but didn't, is that if there were any names on the back, the beginnings of those names would have been cut off when Joe chopped Sarah out of the picture. And sure enough, this is exactly what I was staring at. A list of partial first names and full last names. As I scanned the full last names that were listed, I came up a bit disappointed, as there was no Locker there. All I saw was a bunch of Kellermans. Yet I was sure that the woman I had been taking care of and the woman who had been chopped out of the photo were one and the same, Sarah Locker.

But then I started looking at what remained of the first names, and two of those first names ended in an *H*. In fact, it was the very last two names listed. The first one read *PH*, but the second one just read *H*. I could only assume that the *PH* was for Joseph, Joe's full name. And the last *H*, which appeared by itself, had to be for Sarah. There was no other explanation! According to this photograph, she was a Kellerman. Sarah Kellerman.

Who was she? Was this an eighth sibling I had never known about? Did Joe and Rosalie have a sister named Sarah? I knew about Lilia Kellerman, or at least I knew she had existed. But Sarah Kellerman I had never heard of. No one in the family had ever spoken of a Sarah Kellerman before. I had been under the impression that, perhaps, Sarah was an old girlfriend of Joe's. Now it would seem she was a relative.

Against my better judgment, I walked over to the phone and called Rosalie. She didn't answer, and since she doesn't have an answering machine, I couldn't leave a message. I thought about calling David and Dianne to ask them, since surely, they have the missing piece of this puzzle, but then I thought better of it. I wanted to see them at the funeral, and I was afraid if I started accosting them over the phone regarding his mother's true identity, they wouldn't show up today.

I realized that, at least for the next hour or two, I was left to my own devices, with no one I could reach out to about this. I poured over the photo albums, all of them, hoping I might find some additional answers. But alas, Sarah was nowhere to be found in any of the rest of the pictures, and I wasn't about to remove every single one of them to check the back. There was no way I'd get them back in place before I had to shower and dress for the funeral, and since I was expecting everyone to come back here after the burial for the shiva, I really didn't want a mess of pictures scattered all over the coffee table.

This was really troubling me, but then I looked at the clock and realized I had spent far more time than I had intended to in looking through the albums, and now I was in a pinch. Damn. I got up and made my way back into the bathroom to take a shower, and let me tell you, it seemed like the water took far too long to get warm this morning. I guess it's like that old saying goes. A watched teapot will never boil.

I applied my makeup, got partially dressed, did my hair as best as I could, and then finished dressing with all due speed. I ran back to the kitchen to grab my purse, which wasn't so easy in heels, but at least I didn't fall. With purse in hand, I went into the garage, closed the door behind me, opened the garage door, and got into my car.

I pulled out of the garage, drove down the driveway, and turned onto the street, getting ready to make a left turn at the stop sign to head over to the funeral home. I had about ten minutes to myself on the drive over, which gave me just enough time to get over being rushed to get out the door and to start worrying about the eulogy.

A moment later, I slammed on the brakes! Thank goodness no one was behind me, as they would have plowed right into the rear end of my car. Damn! I forgot to grab the eulogy off the kitchen countertop! Okay, this deserves more than a "Damn!" This deserves a "Well, shit!" I looked at the clock on the dash and realized I really didn't have any time to spare, so after I regained my nerves, I started back down the road to the funeral home.

The parking lot was already starting to fill up by the time I pulled in, so I parked in the first spot I could find and then hightailed it inside. I wish I had had the time to drive around the lot first to see who had already arrived, but I had to settle for just being surprised when I walked into the sanctuary room.

As I entered, all the usual suspects were there. The book club members. The bridge club members. The women's auxiliary of our synagogue. Well, to be fair, there was a pretty big overlap among those groups. Some of Muriel's daughters' longtime friends were there, though they were considerably older than when I had last met them. I probably hadn't seen most of them since Muriel's daughters' weddings.

I recognized some of Morty's old business acquaintances whom I had met at various parties over the years. Joe had known many of them as well. It was like a reunion of the financial fossils, I tell you! Wheelchairs, walkers, and canes littered the place. It took all of the willpower I had not to go up to some of them right then and there and ask them if they had known about Morty's infidelities over the years.

As I got closer to the front of the room where Muriel lay in her wooden casket, I noticed Sarah and David and Dianne on one side of the aisle, and Pete and Lilia on the other side. Lilia and Sarah were just staring at each other. Clearly some form of recognition was occurring, though I wasn't sure to what extent the wheels in their minds were turning. But they knew each other. That much was certain, even if they didn't know how or when. I was just glad Sarah seemed to be dealing with the funeral as well as could be expected.

In the next row on the same side as David, Dianne, and Sarah were some folks I didn't recognize. But when I turned back to Pete and Lilia's side, there were Richard and another man who must have been his date. Whoever heard of bringing a date to a funeral? I mean, sure, I had invited Tripp, though I had also thought better of it! But what I found more interesting was the look Pete was giving the two of them from behind, not that they seemed to notice. I almost thought to stop and to make the introductions, but the timing didn't seem appropriate, so I continued on my way up the aisle.

Two rows later, I saw the traitors. Rosalie and Phyllis. Bernie was there, too, and since he's probably in on the conspiracy to keep me in the dark as well, he's also a traitor. The three traitors. Almost seems like there should be a candy bar named after them. But instead of gooey mousse covered in a chocolate coating, the bar is full of razor blades just waiting to make their way down your digestive track to stab you in the gut, repeatedly.

I gave them all one good, icy stare and continued walking. If they thought even for an instant that I was going to sit with them, they were in for a rude awakening. Fortunately for me, I didn't have to sit alone. Muriel's daughters had made it clear that they wanted me to sit with them in the front row. I don't know if this was out of any true affection for me, or if they just wanted to show their gratitude for my help in making all of the arrangements for today. Hell, I damn near organized the whole thing myself! I'd have been insulted if they *didn't* ask me to do them the honor of sitting with them.

But before I could reach the front row, someone came up

behind me and yanked on the shoulder of my suit. Thank goodness I was wearing shoulder pads, or the offender could have really hurt me. I turned around and came face-to-face with Rosalie. She was wearing a black single-button pantsuit, with a collared white blouse underneath and low heels. Oh, how very modern of her. She looked like a career girl herself!

Well, Rosalie asked me if we could find somewhere to chat privately for a few moments before the funeral service started. I told her she needn't bother and that I had pretty much figured everything out. Yes, I was exaggerating a bit, but she didn't need to know that. One way or the other, I'd have all the answers I needed soon enough. As I turned away from her, she grabbed me again and stared very intently into my eyes, probably trying to determine whether I was being truthful with her. With pure venom in my voice, I told her to go sit back down and that I would deal with her later.

I turned away and headed to the front, where I took my seat among Muriel's family members. Her daughters again expressed their gratitude for my help during this trying time, and I was more than happy to accept their thanks. At least someone appreciated me! We made small talk for the next few moments.

Phyllis came up to the front row and told me in no uncertain terms that she needed to speak to me right away. I told her to fuck off. Yes, I actually told my own daughter to fuck off. Never did I ever think those words would pass through my lips, but well, they just did! She turned around in a tizzy and walked away. Muriel's family looked aghast at me, but I reassured them that Phyllis and I have a very casual relationship. I told them that hardly a day goes by when one of us isn't telling the other to go fuck off. They looked skeptical.

The rabbi took to the bimah a few moments later. A bimah

The Enlightenment of Esther

is what we Jews call a stage in any sort of religious setting. Once he started speaking, I figured I had a good ten to fifteen minutes to try and reconstruct my eulogy in my head. I knew I wanted to talk about Muriel in a way that would do her life the justice that it so deserves. But try as I might, I had a difficult time getting past the cruelty of the events leading up to her death—that at eighty-nine, she had to choose between working or allowing her late husband's reputation to be destroyed.

I tried thinking about all of the wonderful times I had spent with Muriel, pouring over books we've read and beating the pants off her at bridge. I thought about some of the charitable work that she had done. She did Meals on Wheels for ten years straight, until her eyesight got so bad she couldn't find the houses anymore. She also sponsored children living in poor countries through one of those international programs, the name of which escapes me at the moment.

And I would be remiss in not mentioning her devotion to our synagogue. Whatever needed doing, she did it. And she did it with a smile. Years ago, she even taught Sunday school. Muriel believed so strongly that our children are our future. Personally, I think she would have done more good teaching in the public school system than as a Sunday school teacher, but she didn't ask me for my opinion.

I stole a glance back at Phyllis and Rosalie for a moment. Phyllis was seething, and Rosalie seemed a bit defeated. I put a little smirk on my face and turned back around just in time to hear the rabbi announce that a dear friend of Muriel's would be speaking now. He then gestured to me to come on up. I got up from my seat and made my way up to where the rabbi stood. He put an arm around me, introduced me to the congregants, and then took a seat behind me.

27

"My name is Esther Kellerman, and I want to thank everyone here today for coming to pay your respects to my dear friend Muriel Schwartz. It warms my heart to see so many people have turned out for her funeral, and I know her family really appreciates your attendance and your condolences.

"When they asked me to give a eulogy today, I didn't know what I was going to say. And to be honest, I still don't know since I accidentally left what I had written down at home this morning. Muriel deserves better than this, but as I have learned from her death and the events leading up to it, things don't always work out the way you plan for them to. And sometimes you just have to wing it.

"My dear friend Muriel has her wings now, and I hope she is looking down upon us, truly gratified by the outpouring of sympathy and grief over our collective loss. For she was and is a true angel: always willing to help someone in need, always eager to spare hurt feelings when possible, even to her own detriment at times.

The Enlightenment of Esther

"Was Muriel perfect? No. She couldn't see worth a damn towards the end, and it wouldn't surprise me one bit if I were to find out she had bribed an official at the Bureau of Motor Vehicles the last time her license was up for renewal. Muriel had her own way of doing things, and sometimes I would disagree with her decisions, but I always knew that everything she said and did came from love. Love of her husband. Love of her daughters and grandchildren. And love of her fellow men and women."

I took a brief pause here to gauge the reaction of the congregants to what I was saying thus far.

"Those of you who were closest to Muriel know that she was as honest as the day is long. In fact, in the fifty-some years that I knew her, I only ever knew of one secret that she had kept from me. And to my great sadness, it took her years to divulge that secret to me. A secret that not even her daughters knew about," I said, as I pointed to them.

"And if she had told me sooner, she might indeed still be alive today. It was this secret that she was trying to protect that was her eventual undoing. Folks, I hate to break this to you, but Morty Schwartz was an adulterer."

Muriel's daughters looked at me in shock. One of them started to speak, but I held my hand up to stop her. I wasn't done yet. Far from it.

"You see," I continued, "he had a years-long affair with another woman, an affair Muriel knew nothing about until the alleged offspring of said affair knocked on her door one day after Morty passed away. Now you might be wondering why the alleged offspring showed up at all, but bear with me please. All will be revealed."

I looked out into the congregants, and I noticed Pete and Lilia sitting there, stone-faced.

"Pete," I said. "Would you be so kind as to stand up and introduce yourself?"

Pete did not oblige, so I stepped down off of the bimah and headed his way. He was going to do what I told him to do, come hell or high water. When I got to him, I reached over Lilia and grabbed him by the lapel of his suit and yanked him up to a standing position. And then with all the strength I could muster behind my voice, I introduced him to everyone myself.

Muriel's daughters were up out of their seats in a split-second and made a beeline over to us, arms flailing about and voices rising in pitch. Pete made an attempt to block them from getting to Lilia, but I yanked him out into the aisle and stood in front of Lilia myself to protect her. Muriel's daughters started in on Pete, but I again put my hand up and told them to shut their mouths because I had one question that I wanted Pete to answer before I would allow them their chance to pounce on him.

"Pete," I began. "Once and for all, are you or are you not the son of Morty Schwartz?"

He looked at me and then looked at Muriel's daughters, and told everyone that no he wasn't Morty's son.

"Who was your father?" I asked him.

"My father's name was Archie. Archie Matthews."

Out of the corner of my eye, I could see Rosalie just put her head in her hands. Bingo! She recognized the name as the suitor of her sister. My suspicions have been confirmed.

"Now, Pete," I continued. "Explain to Muriel's daughters why you showed up at her doorstep, knowing that their father was not yours as well."

Pete did as he was told. He explained about losing his high-paying job and having to care for his mother and that when the checks stopped coming from Morty, he got desperate. He explained to them that he had threatened their mother with the exposure of their late father's infidelity if she didn't continue to pay.

"And that," I said to Muriel's daughters, "is why your mother at eighty-nine years old started caretaking for a neighbor with dementia. To earn the money she needed to pay Pete off. She was trying to protect your father's reputation, and it literally killed her to do so."

The next thing I knew, Muriel's older daughter was screaming at Pete, and the younger one was slapping him across the face.

"So my mother is dead now because you couldn't take care of yours!" the older one accused.

The younger sister then added, "You'll be hearing from our lawyer!"

"Well, dears," I said to the both of them, "I have to point out that if you were more involved in your mother's life, you might have known about her dire financial situation. She had to either sell the house or find some other way to earn the money to pay Pete off. I mean, when you really get right down to it, this is all your fault for keeping your distance from your mother for so many years."

That shut them up! But before I could say anything else, Richard turned around from the row ahead with a disgusted look on his face.

"So, Pete," he snarled. "You pretended to be so high and mighty with me, but you had no problems stringing along a poor old widow woman for money. Looks like I definitely made the right call in dumping your sorry ass!"

Well, that was a twist I wasn't expecting.

"Richard, you're misremembering. Must be all those meds you're taking now. Let me refresh your memory. You cheated on me, got infected with AIDS, and didn't tell me. I had to find out from your doctor! Incidentally, does your date here know that you're HIV-positive?" Pete asked, pointing to the man sitting next to Richard.

The man sitting next to Richard nodded, a bit embarrassed.

"Thank you very much, Pete," Richard fumed. "Half of my clientele is literally sitting in this room, and you've just outed my status to all of them!"

I noticed out of the corner of my eye that a couple sitting to Richard's left started scooting away from him.

"Oh, for heaven's sake!" I yelled at them. "You can't catch it just from sitting next to someone!"

They demurred and stopped inching away from Richard. Well, at least now I know why he's been looking so thin lately.

"Pete?" I asked, turning my attention away from Richard, "do you have it too?"

"No, I was always a top—" he started.

"Spare me the details!" I quickly interrupted before he could get another word in edgewise.

You know, I considered myself to be an enlightened woman, but I wasn't *that* enlightened.

"Pete, I just have one more question for you now. What is your mother Lilia's maiden name?" I asked, pointing towards her.

He and Lilia looked at each other for a moment, and she nodded her consent.

"Kellerman," he said flatly.

Well, Phyllis's head snapped around and Rosalie started moaning. Double bingo! While Rosalie and Phyllis were in cahoots over keeping me in the dark about Sarah's true identity, it's clear that Rosalie did not include Phyllis in on her knowl-

The Enlightenment of Esther

edge of Lilia's existence. As expected, both of them rose from their seats and started making their way towards us.

Meanwhile, Muriel's daughters tried to start in on Pete again, but I told them that if they knew what was good for them, they'd go back to their seats in the front row. When they hesitated, I shouted at them to move their asses, or I'd move their asses for them! You know, it just occurred to me that I've been doing quite a bit of swearing lately. I'd have to keep an eye on that. I'd hate for this new habit to get out of control! But I wasn't done with swearing quite yet.

As Rosalie approached with Phyllis in tow, she squinted her eyes at Lilia, probably trying to see if the seventy-something-year-old woman sitting before her now bore any resemblance to the beautiful girl she remembered.

"Ladies and gentlemen," I said as loudly as I could for all to hear. "This is my late husband's sister Rosalie. And this is Lilia, their long-lost baby sister. A sister whom everyone in the family had always told me was dead!"

You could have heard a pin drop in the room. No one said a word.

"Well?" I asked Rosalie. "Don't just stand there! Go hug your long-lost sister!"

But she didn't. What happened next was pretty remarkable, though. Lilia stood up, holding on to the back of the row in front of her, and with a little help from Pete and myself, made her way into the aisle where Rosalie still stood. She took her one good arm and wrapped it around Rosalie, who in turn embraced her as if her life depended on it. I tell you, this was a made-for-a-Kodak-commercial moment.

Phyllis tried to put her arm around me in some sort of attempt to share the tenderness of this moment. I whispered in her ear that I wasn't done with her yet. She then promptly removed her arm from my back.

"What I don't understand," I said so that everyone could hear. "Is why? Why did Lilia leave the family? And why did the family then pretend she was dead? Hell, they even sat shiva for her!"

Okay, so clearly I should have asked these questions privately because Lilia hadn't known that her family had actually sat shiva for her. She pulled away from Rosalie and looked directly into her eyes.

"Lilia," Rosalie started to explain, "you know how things were back then. But there isn't a day that goes by that I don't regret what happened and how we all handled the situation. Maybe it wouldn't have mattered so much today, but back in those times, things were very different."

"Wait," I interjected. "Pete, did you lie before when you told Muriel and me that you weren't biracial? Was your father black? Is that why the family didn't approve?"

So then I had to explain to everyone in the room that Muriel had initially thought that Pete was biracial. I have to admit that this was getting a little embarrassing, but I've come too far to stop now. And then I realized my mistake. I had seen a picture of Pete's father the other day when Rosalie was taking me on her photographic stroll down memory lane. I was absolutely sure he was the man standing next to Lilia in that last photograph Rosalie had of her. He definitely wasn't black.

"Damn," I said. I just embarrassed myself in front of all of these people for nothing.

"Pete," I continued. "I know your father wasn't black. Never mind how I know that, but suffice it to say, I do. Now, would you be so kind as to give me the missing piece of this puzzle now?"

He looked at his mother Lilia, and then at his newly discovered aunt Rosalie, probably hoping one of them would speak up so that he wouldn't have to. Well, it was wishful thinking on his part that his mother would be able to articulate well enough to answer me. And it was beyond foolish of him to think Rosalie would voluntarily divulge whatever secret it is that they were all keeping.

After a couple of seconds passed, I said, "I don't think either of these two are going to come to your rescue, Pete, so you might as well get on with it. Tell me why your mother left the family and why your aunt and the rest of the family sat shiva for her."

"Archie Matthews wasn't Jewish," he responded.

28

"So? What's that got to do with anything?" I asked. But as soon as the words escaped my lips, I realized exactly what Archie's religion had to do with this whole mess.

I looked at Rosalie in disbelief. She couldn't even look me in the eye. Somewhere in the background, I heard Muriel's daughters causing a ruckus over what they were calling the desecration of their mother's funeral. I turned around and told them that I didn't understand why they cared more about their mother in death than they did in life. Well, that shut them up. Hopefully for good.

Turning back to Rosalie, I asked, "Do you want to explain what happened now? Or should I just tell you what I think went down all those years ago?"

"This really isn't the time or the place, Esther," Rosalie replied.

"Oh, but I think it is," I said. And then turning to the rest of the congregants, I asked, "Don't you all agree?"

I made sure my tone communicated the rhetorical intent of

The Enlightenment of Esther

my question. I figured since I arranged for this whole day of mourning, I'd run it as I saw fit. And if it took the rest of the day, I was going to get my answers.

"Fine, Esther," Rosalie snapped. "Far be it for you to just let the cards lay where they fell. Incidentally, you're not as good of a bridge player as you think you are. I've been meaning to tell you that for years, and it feels good to get that off my chest!"

"Now wait just a damn minute, Rosalie. I . . . wait . . . don't you change the subject now. Spill it!"

"Oh, all right, Esther," she responded. "If you insist on me publicly shaming myself, not to mention your late husband, Joe, then so be it. Yes, Archie Matthews wasn't Jewish. Yes, he asked Lilia to marry him. Yes, our family told her in no uncertain terms that she was prohibited from marrying a gentile. And yes, when she ran off with him in protest, we sat shiva for her. She was dead to us."

Both Rosalie and Lilia started tearing up, probably for different reasons, though. What we really needed now was a psychologist, but since I doubted there was one, I went for the next best thing.

"Oh, Rabbi!" I shouted back towards the front of the room. "Would you mind coming down off of the bimah for a moment? I think we're in need of your expertise over here."

He shook his head and said that this was really a family matter that he didn't feel comfortable involving himself in. Well, I told him that I didn't feel particularly comfortable making my monthly pledge to the synagogue's building fund either, and that maybe I would discontinue making those payments in the very near future. As you can imagine, that got him up off his tuchus pretty damn quick. He reached us in mere seconds. Oh, and the word "tuchus" is how we Jews refer to one's rear end, in case you weren't familiar.

"Thank you, Rabbi, for so graciously agreeing to come down off of your perch to help us here. I'm sure you could impart some sage words of wisdom to Rosalie and Lilia at this time. And if you can't, I'll write them down for you and you can just read them."

This last was my attempt to communicate to the rabbi what I wanted him to say. I had only my faith in his understanding of the financial situation of the synagogue, should I pull back my support, to guide him towards the right approach here. I hated to use money to strong-arm anyone into doing anything. Well, unless it involves me staying out of jail. But I was at my rope's end.

"Rosalie, Lilia," the rabbi began. "I know that you both are in a world of hurt right now. One sister choosing the path of love. The other choosing the path of faith. One sister wishing the family would support her. The other toeing the line. Two diametrically opposed approaches to love and faith. If you'll permit me, I'd like to reflect on your dilemma a bit and study the scriptures a bit more before giving my advice."

He turned around to head back up the aisle to the bimah, but I grabbed his suit jacket to stop him, and well, I ripped a gaping hole where the shoulder meets—met—the left sleeve. He whipped around to face me in fury, but he was no match for Esther Kellerman. No sir.

"What are you going to do, Rabbi? Stand up there and read the Torah aloud to all of us? Hell, there isn't even a Torah anywhere to be found in this funeral home. Just speak from your heart! You must have counseled hundreds of families during the course of your career. I know you've got the knowledge and experience to deal with this situation right here and right now. And you might as well make an effort at it before I lose my temper and rip the other sleeve off of your jacket."

The Enlightenment of Esther

The rabbi decided to heed my advice and made another attempt at smoothing things over between Rosalie and Lilia.

"In biblical times, it was important to keep Jews from marrying and/or having children with non-Jews. It was all part of building a Jewish nation one day in the promised land. You know that the Jewish bloodline is passed down through the mother, so that each baby born to a Jewish mother was in fact Jewish as well."

"Yeah, yeah, yeah," I said to the rabbi. "Get to the point about it being less important in the here and now."

"Right, well, it's like this," he said to Rosalie. "Umm, if Moses could fall in love with an Egyptian princess five thousand years ago, then I think God has given your sister a pass on falling in love and marrying a gentile."

"Really, Rabbi?" I interjected. "That's the best you can do? Maybe you should try a little harder."

"I'd rather not," he responded, rather forcefully. "Look, I'm a rabbi, not a politician. I can't just read into a teleprompter that's being fed from a connection to your mind, Mrs. Kellerman. So whatever it is that you want me to say, it really would be better coming from you directly."

"Fine," I snipped. "Go back to your seat and pray for some brains."

He went off to his perch in a huff.

Turning back to Rosalie and Lilia, I said, "It's time to bury the hatchet. This is the first time you've seen each other in nearly sixty years. I'm no theologian, but I believe truly in my heart that everything happens for a reason. And there's a reason you two have found your way back to each other, even if it was through me and my meddling. Look, I can't force you to mend fences, but I can promise you this. If you don't, you will both regret it for the rest of your days."

Rosalie looked at me, tears in her eyes, and then grabbed Lilia's hand.

"You know how our mother was about these things," she said to Lilia. "What she said is what we did. It was always that way. I know you remember that."

Lilia stared back at her, not really sure how to respond. Or perhaps she couldn't respond.

"But I shouldn't have let it happen," she continued. "You were my baby sister, but you were also my little girl," Rosalie continued with genuine emotion. "I loved you like a daughter. But you weren't mine. You were our mother's, and I let her cast you out of the family. I did regret it. I do regret it. All I can do now is hope that you can find it in your heart to forgive me."

Lilia took a moment to decide what to do, and then she embraced her sister Rosalie. I turned to Phyllis to introduce her to her cousin, Pete. The two were cordial to each other, which I guess is about the best I could have expected for now. I love my daughter dearly when she's not stabbing me in the back, but she's definitely not the warm and fuzzy feeling type.

I was too busy focusing on Pete and Phyllis that I didn't notice Lilia break away from Rosalie's embrace and make her way over to where Sarah, David, and Dianne were sitting. She had her walker with her, thankfully, but as soon as Pete noticed what was going on, he rushed over to her side to make sure she didn't stumble and fall.

Rosalie turned around to see where Lilia was headed, and I could see the warm and joyous expression on her face melt away. I took Rosalie by the arm and led her over to where Lilia had stopped in front of the others. It was time for some answers where Sarah was concerned, and I was going to get them one way or the other.

Sarah was sitting closest to the aisle, and David and Dianne were to the right of her. Lilia leaned over a little bit to look directly into Sarah's face, probably wanting to make sure she was looking at the woman she thought she was before saying anything.

"Sarah," Lilia managed to emit.

"I know you," Sarah responded, but she seemed to be having trouble figuring out how.

Lilia looked at Rosalie, and then at me, hoping one of us might be able to help her out a bit. But I was at a loss for words, and Rosalie didn't seem interested in enlightening any of us.

So, I turned to everyone in the room and said, "You all are probably wondering what's going on right now. And so am I. But I can tell you this. This woman sitting here is none other than the same woman that Muriel and I were looking after during these last weeks. Her name is Sarah, and she has a touch of dementia, so you'll have to forgive her if she's having a little trouble with her memory today.

"This is her son, David, and her daughter-in-law, Dianne," I continued, pointing to each of them.

"David and Dianne moved to our neighborhood from Pickerington, and they moved Sarah in with them. She had been living somewhere on the west side of town on her own, but as she was showing signs of mental decline, she could no longer live by herself. So, the three of them moved into our neighborhood all at the same time.

"They introduced themselves to Muriel and me as the Locker family. Sarah Locker, David Locker, and Dianne Locker. I had presumed that Sarah's husband had passed away some years back, even though she kept trying to tell me that he had just run to the corner store for some eggs and would be right back. No one ever told me what his first name was, but I assumed that his last name was Locker. Wouldn't that make the most sense to all of you?" I asked the crowd.

David and Dianne looked aghast at me, and Phyllis kept tugging on my sleeve, probably hoping to divert my attention from my mission at hand. It didn't work.

"Early on in Muriel's and my caretaking of Sarah, I asked her one day if she knew who I was. She had trouble remembering. I then asked her if she knew her own name. She said her name was Sarah Kellerman."

An audible gasp rang through the room. Phyllis tried to drag me away, but I told her to fuck off again. Loud enough for everyone to hear this time. More gasps ensued.

Turning back to the matter at hand, I continued, "Now at the time, I didn't think much of it. I just assumed that she had remembered my own last name and decided it belonged to her as well. I mean, who would have done anything differently in such a situation?

"But more recently, a funny thing happened. Lilia here called me up one day. We were already on friendly terms, as I had been helping her out a bit with getting connected with the appropriate specialists to assess her chances for any further recovery from a stroke she had twenty years ago. She already knew of the situation with Sarah Locker, and she wanted to know if I knew whether the surname Locker was Sarah's married name or her maiden name. I told Lilia that I had assumed it was the former.

"And that may indeed be the case. But what I have since discovered, is that Sarah was also a Kellerman at one point in her life. So, when she told me her name was Sarah Kellerman before, she was actually correct. Now, Kellerman is Rosalie's maiden name, my married name as I was married to her

The Enlightenment of Esther

brother Joe, and Lilia's maiden name as well. So, Rosalie, Joe, and Lilia are all siblings.

"But what I don't know is how Sarah fits into this dysfunctional family tree. Is she yet another long-lost sister that no one in the family ever spoke of? Or perhaps a wayward cousin? Maybe an illegitimate child of someone in the family? All I know is that she's standing next to my late husband in a family photograph from sixty years ago."

"Mom," Phyllis whispered into my ear, "you're getting yourself all worked up. Come sit down and rest for a moment before your blood pressure goes sky high."

"Phyllis!" I said loudly enough for everyone to hear. "I'm not as feeble as you make me out to be. Believe me, whatever is going on here and whatever relation Sarah turns out to be I can handle."

Turning to David, I said, "Since I don't expect to get an honest answer out of any of the other Kellermans here, would you be so kind as to enlighten me on how you, your wife, and your mother fit in to our family?"

He and Dianne gave each other a look and then nodded in agreement.

"My mother, Sarah," he began to say, "was the first wife of your late husband, Joe Kellerman, and I am his son."

29

I must have been having one of those out-of-body experiences. It was if I was looking down upon myself and thinking that there's no way this could possibly be happening. I mean, what woman in her right mind would expect to find out that her husband had had an ex-wife that she herself hadn't known about? This is the stuff of soap operas and bargain-bin novels, not real life.

And yet, here I was, being confronted with the very real prospect that Sarah was indeed Joe's first wife. All I could think of to ask was how. David looked at Rosalie, hoping she would explain the situation, or at least part of it. And to my surprise, she did.

"Esther, what David is saying is true. Sarah was married to Joe," she confirmed.

"But how? When? I mean, how could he possibly have had a first wife and not have told me?" I asked, my head spinning by now.

"Do you really want to know?" Rosalie asked in reply.

She had a point there. Did I really want to know? I think that if today were just a once-in-a-lifetime encounter with Sarah, I might have said no. But since she lives in my neighborhood, and there's no way of getting around that, nor the fact that Phyllis now has a half-brother, I figured we might as well air out all of the dirty laundry right here and right now. I nodded to Rosalie to continue.

"Joe and Sarah were married for several years, before you ever knew him," Rosalie said. "They seemed so happy together, and then one day, she up and left. No note. No explanation."

I looked at David for confirmation of these details, and he nodded back.

Rosalie continued, "Joe searched for her. He even went up to Minneapolis where he knew she was from. The way Joe told it to me, Sarah's parents said they hadn't heard from her and didn't know her whereabouts."

David interjected and informed us that this wasn't actually true. Sarah was indeed at her parents' house, but she told them to lie for her. And that's what they did.

"Esther, dear," Rosalie resumed. "Joe kept searching for her, but after a while, we all figured there was no hope. He was crushed. We all were. Especially since her disappearance had happened so soon after we lost Lilia. I mean, well, we didn't lose Lilia so much as we cut her out of our lives. But we lost Sarah."

"So, Sarah disappeared, and sometime after that he and I met," I reasoned.

"He was so taken by you, Esther," Rosalie offered. "He'd light up at the mention of your name."

"But wait. If Sarah had just disappeared, then how could Joe have married me? I mean, legally?" I asked.

And then it hit me. "Oh my God, I'm a bigamist. I mean, Joe was a bigamist. I mean, he couldn't get a divorce from Sarah if he couldn't find her, right? So he was married to both of us for 49 years and 364 days."

"No, Esther," Rosalie responded. "After he had proposed to you and you had accepted, Joe paid a doctor friend of his to write up a phony death certificate for Sarah. So in the eyes of the law, Joe was no longer married to Sarah. You didn't enter into a bigamous marriage, Esther."

Well, David and Dianne looked aghast at the revelation that Sarah had been declared dead, at least as far as the state of Ohio was concerned. Then, out of nowhere, Sarah stood up and pointed at me. She then proceeded to tell the whole room that I was trying to steal her husband.

"That's her! That husband stealer! She wants my Joe!" Sarah yelled.

All I could say was that at least Sarah could remember her husband's name again. It's just a shame we had to share Joe now. She didn't seem like the sharing type to me. David managed to get her to sit back down after a small but unseemly struggle, though she still kept yelling.

"Wait a minute," I said, cutting Sarah off. "David, you said that you are Joe's son. So, that means your mother, Sarah, was pregnant with you before she left Joe. Did your mother ever tell you whether he knew about the pregnancy before she left?"

"No, your husband and my father didn't know that my mother was pregnant when she left."

I stole a quick glance at Rosalie and Phyllis to see how they were reacting to what David had just confirmed. The expressions on their faces told me all I needed to know. None of this was news to either of them. Figures.

"Did your mother even know she was pregnant at the time?" I asked, turning back towards David.

"Yes, my mother knew she was pregnant with me. It's ultimately why she decided to leave."

"But why? Why would any woman, especially in those times, leave her husband if she knew she was pregnant with his child?" I asked. None of this was making any sense to me.

David hesitated in responding, and it would seem that Rosalie and Phyllis were just as perplexed as I was. So perhaps they weren't completely in the know after all. Serves them right!

"We're waiting on pins and needles for your response, David," I said.

I then broke out into song, humming the *Final Jeopardy* theme. This drew some chuckles from the congregants, but more importantly, it worked in getting David to answer me.

"My mother, Sarah, isn't Jewish."

You know, I've experienced déjà vu more times than I care to remember, but never have I experienced it in such close proximity to the original event. I had to grab on to the end of the row where Sarah, David, and Dianne were sitting just to keep from falling. My head literally hurt.

"Esther," David said, "I know this is a lot to take in, and I'm sorry for that. My mother pretended she was Jewish because she was so in love with Joe. The pretending part wasn't difficult for her to do because she had known many Jews in Minneapolis. She was able to claim the stories of those she knew as her own, and created a whole new past for herself that bore little resemblance to reality. And whatever she didn't know, she picked up quickly, even learning how to keep a kosher house."

"Joe never cared about keeping a kosher house, at least not by the time I met him," I informed David.

"Esther," Rosalie cut in, "he was so taken with you. He wasn't about to let anything get in the middle of the two of you.

In fact, when he first told us about you, my mother asked him if you were Jewish. He said that you were, but that even if you weren't, he didn't care. He'd run off like Lilia did if he had to."

Lilia's face brightened a bit upon hearing this. As for me, I didn't know how to feel about all of this. Part of me was seething at Joe for being a part of Lilia's banishment from the family and Sarah's subsequent flight. But then again, if Sarah hadn't done what she did, I never would have met Joe myself. And what a wonderful 49 years and 364 days of marriage we had together. I wouldn't trade those years for the world.

David continued, "My mother was always prepared for the truth to come out one way or another. But when she discovered that she was pregnant, and after what had happened with Lilia, she realized that should the truth come out, there was no way she'd allow for anyone to reject me as a result of my not being Jewish. She felt that if she had stayed and given birth to me here, that my father would reject me if he discovered we weren't Jewish. My mother couldn't bear the thought of that. And that's why she left."

"So you're saying that Sarah left to protect you. To protect you from what she thought would happen if Joe discovered that both she and you weren't Jewish."

"Yes. That about sums it up," David replied.

"And how did you find out about all of this? I mean, why did your mother finally decide to tell you the truth about your father and my husband?" I asked.

"To tell you the truth, I don't think she ever meant to. But as her dementia started to progress, I suspect she just forgot to continue keeping this secret from me. Dianne and I had gone over to her house for dinner one Saturday night, and we were all taking various strolls down memory lane at the dinner table. Somehow, we got onto the subject of deceased relatives, namely my grandparents. And with a very curious look on her face, my mother said that she was wondering what ever happened to Joe. When I asked her who Joe was, she said, 'Oh, you know who he is.' Well, no I didn't, so I asked her again, and that's when she said, 'Your father.'"

That must have come as quite a shock to him, I thought.

"Up until then," David continued, "the only information I could ever get out of her regarding who my father was was that he was a casual acquaintance of hers. She would always maintain that they had just the one night together, and then he was gone for good. She would say that she barely knew him."

I looked down at Sarah to see if I could ascertain how much of this conversation she was following. I saw tears rolling down her cheeks. What she was remembering I wasn't quite sure, but I took hold of her hand and gave it a squeeze. She looked up at me, a knowing look in her eyes. But I decided not to press my luck and chose not to say anything. I'll always choose to remember this moment as a connection between the two of us, with a shared knowledge of a husband we both had loved. A husband we both had lost.

A new question arose in my mind though. I asked David how long ago was this fateful dinner where Sarah spilled the beans.

"About eight months ago. She was getting pretty forgetful, but she was still living on her own."

"But tell me this, when did Sarah come back to Columbus? How old were you?"

David sighed and confessed to the fact that neither Sarah nor he had returned to Columbus until they moved in to my neighborhood. So she had never lived on the west side of Columbus, and he and Dianne had never lived in Pickerington.

They had all moved straight from Minneapolis to just down the street from me less than two months ago.

"So," I continued, "your mother accidentally let slip that Joe was your father. Then what?"

"I hired an investigator to find out where he was, if he was still in Columbus, and how his life had turned out. Did he remarry? Did he have other children?"

"And I assume the investigator found out that Joe had passed away."

"Yes, but the investigator told me that Rosalie was still living and informed me of your existence and that I had a half-sister, Phyllis."

"And what did you do with that information?" I asked, figuring I probably already knew.

"I called Aunt Rosalie and introduced myself," David responded.

Knowing Rosalie as well as I do, I was pretty sure how that conversation went. David confirmed my suspicions when he said that Rosalie had been willing to give any further information that he wanted on the family but wasn't interested in meeting him or talking with him any further. My guess is she was trying to protect me from having to find out that Joe had been married once before.

Well, Rosalie's plan backfired as he called her again a few months ago to let her know that the three of them were moving to Columbus and into our neighborhood. Phyllis added that Rosalie had then called her in a frantic panic and explained the situation to her. So, this is where Phyllis entered the scheme. Both of them knew they were eventually going to have to tell me about Sarah, but I think each was hoping that the other would take the bullet.

Turning to Rosalie and Phyllis, I reasoned, "And neither of

you had counted on me actually meeting Sarah and involving myself in her day-to-day life, thanks to Muriel. But once I was, why didn't one of you tell me? You must have known I'd find out one way or the other on my own."

"David swore to me," Rosalie chimed in, "that he would allow us to tell you ourselves. Admittedly, he was growing impatient with us as the weeks went by, but he kept his word."

"You slipped up, Rosalie, when you showed me that photograph from your mother's second wedding," I commented.

"Yup, I sure did!" Rosalie laughed, though I didn't find it so funny.

"I hope you can find it in your heart to forgive us," Phyllis said.

David then extended an invitation to all of us to have dinner sometime, including Pete and Lilia. And then a feeling of dread started in the pit of my stomach at the mention of food. I quickly looked down at my watch, and realized I still had time.

"Well, shit," I said to everyone in the room. "I forgot to arrange for someone to be at my house to take delivery on the food for the shiva. I gotta run! See everyone at the shiva! If you need the address or directions, just ask Phyllis or Rosalie!"

30

I had arrived home just in time to take delivery on the refreshments, and thankfully, I had managed to get everything set up right as the first guests were arriving from the cemetery. Whether there was enough to go around would remain to be seen, however. Usually, shivas aren't advertised to everyone in attendance at a funeral, but I was in such a rush to get out of there that I wasn't thinking clearly. So far, the food seemed to be holding up well.

Out of the corner of my eye, I spotted Muriel's daughters and their families all huddled together, so I decided to go over and make my apologies. I know Muriel loved her family, and they loved her in return, even if they were a bit too absent from her life in my opinion. They expressed their gratitude again for my help in planning everything today, and I in turn told them that I wouldn't have had it any other way. Yes, that was a little white lie on my part, but I figured it didn't cost me anything and wasn't going to hurt anyone.

Not far from Muriel's family sat Pete and Richard on a sofa

together. It looked like the two of them had a lot to discuss, so I decided to discreetly eavesdrop for a moment. Well, subtlety isn't one of my strong suits, and they both noticed me listening in. What else could I do but squeeze the two of them apart and make a spot for myself in the middle? So, that's exactly what I did. I grabbed both of their hands, which surprised Richard I guess because of the AIDS thing, and told them both what I thought.

"I think there's still love there between the two of you. I can see it in all four of your eyes. Oh sure, there's anger too. But I'm going to let you in on a little secret from someone who's lived a good deal longer than either of you. The opposite of love isn't hate. It's indifference, and I think what happened at the funeral earlier proves that neither of you is indifferent towards the other. I don't know much about gay relationships, but I do know a thing about love, and honeys, you've got it in spades for each other. It's a small world, and we can't just avoid those we've hurt or who have hurt us until the end of time. Talk to each other. I promise you both will find some sense of peace in your hearts if you do."

They looked at each other with tenderness and love, and I knew that my work here was done. So I got back up and started towards the kitchen counter to do another food supply check. But then a thought occurred to me. I wonder what had happened to Richard's date from the funeral. I started to turn around and walk back over to Richard to ask him, but I decided to let sleeping dogs lie. It's really none of my business anyway. Not that that has ever stopped me before, but perhaps it's time for me to turn over a new leaf. Oh, who am I kidding? I'm old, set in my ways, and there's no changing me now!

I walked over to the breakfast table where Rosalie, Lilia, and Sarah were sitting together. It dawned on me that today was the first time in sixty years that the three of them had been in the same room together, let alone sitting at the same table. They were all smiling at each other, Rosalie and Sarah talking over each other, and Lilia trying to get a word in edgewise. While I couldn't say definitively, it seemed as though enough of Sarah's long-term memory was still intact to appreciate this moment for what it truly was. A miracle. She clearly recognized both Rosalie and Lilia.

"Rosalie," I said as I took a seat next to her, "I don't think I've ever seen you looking so positively radiant. It really suits you. You should try asking for forgiveness for your transgressions more often!"

"Oh, don't be silly, Esther. No eighty-five-year-old ever looks radiant," she replied.

Well, I had to laugh at that, for she was right. No amount of moisturizer or makeup can hide the footprints of time's march across our faces. But for the first time in a long while, there really was a peaceful glow to her, and it warmed my heart to no end.

"How are you feeling, Sarah?" I asked, bracing myself for her answer.

"I'm fine. How are you, dear?" she asked.

"I'm doing well. Thank you for asking. Are you enjoying this little family reunion? It's been awhile since you've seen Rosalie and Lilia," I responded.

"Oh, really?" she asked. "How long has it been?"

"Nearly sixty years," I informed Sarah.

"I must be really old then," she laughed.

"We're all really old," Rosalie added.

"Lilia," I began, "tell me what Rosalie was like all those years ago. I mean, as your older sister."

The Enlightenment of Esther

"Bossy!" she said, to which we all chuckled, and then added with a wink, "Best sister ever."

"And to think, if it hadn't been for my meddling, you all might not have ever seen each other again! Someone should give me an award. An Oscar for best meddler ever!" I said.

"Well, don't count your chickens before they hatch," Rosalie admonished. "You remember my mother, don't you? Your mother-in-law? If meddling were an Olympic sport, she'd have taken home a gold medal."

Lilia and I both nodded in agreement, but Sarah seemed a little puzzled. I guess her long-term memory could only get her so far on a stroll down memory lane. I can't say I blame her, though. My mother-in-law was quite a handful, and it's probably to Sarah's benefit not to remember her.

I sat there for a few more moments, listening to the three of them chat with each other with varying degrees of success. I still had some questions I wanted answered. Like what happened to Archie Matthews? How did he die? When did he die? How did Sarah become a hairdresser? Did she and David live with her parents throughout his childhood? Why had Lilia not made any attempts to reunite with the family over these nearly sixty years? Even after her mother passed away? But I decided now was not the time to pry. Every good meddler knows how and when to pick her opportunities, and this wasn't one of them.

My stomach started rumbling, so I got up and fixed myself a small plate. I was going to sit back down with Rosalie, Lilia, and Sarah, but I reminded myself that a good host must circulate the room. David, Dianne, Phyllis, and Bernie were all standing in the far corner of the living room, so I made my way over to join them.

"Well, David," I began, "it looks like I'm actually your step-mother, and not just your oh-so-caring but meddlesome neighbor. Now, what should you call me? Mom? Ma? Mother?"

"I'll probably just stick with Esther," he laughed. "I do think my own mother might get a little confused if she were to hear me calling you by any of the names you suggested."

"Probably so," I agreed. "Oh, and Dianne, I suppose that makes you my step-daughter-in-law. Welcome to the family!"

"Thank you, Esther," Dianne said. "I want to thank you for everything you've done for us with Sarah. And for welcoming us into the family. I can't begin to imagine what a shock it was to find out that Joe had been married once before."

"Well, yes, it was. But I'm going to let you in on a little life secret I've learned along the way. You just have to keep on keeping on."

Apparently I was giving away life's secrets left and right today.

"I couldn't have put it better myself," Phyllis interjected. "I hope you can forgive me for keeping all of this from you, Mom."

"Yes, of course, dear. Misguided though you were, I do realize you were just trying to protect me," I replied.

"And what about you, Bernie?" I asked. "How much of all of this did you know about?"

"As much as my wife did, I'm afraid," he responded. "I did a little digging when we first heard about Sarah and was able to locate that forged death certificate for her. I'm glad I did, because we were a little worried that, without a divorce on record, there might have been some legal implications involving your marriage to Joe. But rest assured, there's nothing to worry about."

"Glad to hear it," I added, thinking how precarious my situation could have been otherwise.

I looked over to Pete and Richard and gestured for them to

The Enlightenment of Esther

come over and join us. Pete is David's and Phyllis's cousin, after all, and I figured they should all get acquainted. Once I made the introductions, not that they were really necessary at this point, I took my leave of the group and went off to refill my plate.

As I walked around and gazed at all of the people gathered in my home, seeing old friends get reacquainted and newly known family members begin to forge bonds with one another, my heart was content. When you get down to it, really, family is about those with whom you surround yourself. And if a family can make you rich, I'm the richest woman in the world.

Someone tapped my shoulder a moment later, and I turned around to see who the offending finger belonged to. He was an older gentleman, perhaps in his mid-eighties, about my height, and nearly a full head of white hair. I didn't recognize him.

"Mrs. Kellerman," he started. "I want to express my deep condolences to you on the loss of your friend Muriel. I'm sure she's giving Morty a piece of her mind right now!"

"Thank you for that," I offered. "I'm afraid to admit that I don't recognize your face. Do we know each other?"

"No, we don't," he replied.

"Then may I ask your name?"

"Sure, of course. Where are my manners? My name is Nathan Levinovich."

"The name doesn't ring a bell," I said.

"Ahh, well, when I was working, I used to go by the name Nat Levinson."

ALSO BY JOSHUA BERKOV

Adulting at the Moto-Lodge: A Humorous Family Life Romp

A self-assured man. A meddlesome motel owner. A cascade of disasters that could end in healing... or catapult him into yet another fiasco.

Rob Cunningham believes he can do no wrong. So when his wife kicks him to the curb for cheating with her sister, the serial philanderer still refuses to emerge from his cocoon of self-love. But when the smug salesman loses his job and needs a new gig, he's appalled to discover he's at the mercy of his eccentric landlady's haphazard puppeteering.

As the strange circumstances of Rob's handyman handiwork force him to confront issues from his troubled childhood, he grudgingly admits he isn't a flawless human being. And as his new friend spills the beans on old secrets, he risks dipping a tentative toe into the waters of reconciliation.

Will Rob's carnival of calamities be the wake-up call he needs to transform his world?

Adulting at the Moto-Lodge is a humorous standalone novel. If you like irreverent observations on humanity, dysfunctional families, and plenty of laugh-out-loud moments, then you'll adore Joshua Berkov's lighthearted mosaic.

The Enlightenment of Angeline

Angeline Sims is no shrinking violet. She's tough, opinionated, bossy, and she's got a bone to pick with nearly everyone in her life. Set in the fictitious Eastern North Carolina small town of Shelbington, Angeline has been given a terminal diagnosis, with mere months left to live.

Upon learning of this news, her adult children and grandchildren come home for one last visit. There is no love lost between any of the family members, and they all have secrets that they voluntarily or involuntarily reveal throughout the course of the novel, culminating in an explosive family dinner at which the biggest bombshells are dropped.

The Nasty Lady Librarian of Shelbington

A hilarious prequel novella to The Enlightenment of Angeline.

Southern small-town retired library director Evelyn Williams finds herself suddenly unretired when her corrupt replacement is summarily dismissed by the library's board. When Evelyn returns for her first day back on the job, she's appalled at the state she finds the library in. Books are misplaced. Tables are overturned. And to make matters worse, most of the library staff fails to show up on her first day back. With only a well-meaning but naïve temp by her side, Evelyn must contend with the challenges of restoring the library to its former glory. But, can she? Or will this job prove too difficult even for her, especially given the penchant her replacement's allies have for sabotage?

The Nasty Lady Librarian of Shelbington is a welcome return to small-town drama for fans of Joshua Berkov's first novel The Enlightenment of Angeline. Several notable characters from the novel make appearances in this novella including Angeline herself! And if you haven't read The Enlightenment of Angeline, pull up a chair, pour yourself a glass of sweet tea and enjoy this introduction to the laugh-out-loud shenanigans of the residents of Shelbington, North Carolina.

Shelbington Sweets: A Humorous Short Story

Seventy-five-year-old Eugenia Thompson thinks it's time for a change in her life. After losing her husband last year to a short illness, she decides to mortgage her house and open up a cupcake shop in her hometown of Shelbington, North Carolina. What could possibly go wrong, she wonders? Well, for starters, Eugenia's part-time helper calls out sick on opening day, forcing her to hire a temp on very short notice. She then wonders whether her business will succeed when the avalanche of customers she was expecting doesn't materialize. Will Eugenia survive her first day in business, or will she face financial ruin?

Shelbington Sweets is a short-story companion to the author's delightfully humorous first novel *The Enlightenment of Angeline*. A number of the novel's most endearing characters make appearances throughout the story.

ABOUT THE AUTHOR

Joshua Berkov is a librarian by day and a writer by night. He holds a BA in Philosophy from Brown University, an MSLS from the University of North Carolina at Chapel Hill, and an MBA from East Carolina University. He lives with his partner and two cats in Raleigh, North Carolina, though he is originally from Los Angeles, California. Josh is an avid reader and enjoys exploring new authors and genres regularly. Nothing gives him greater pleasure than to make those around him laugh out loud.

Made in the USA
Coppell, TX
07 October 2022